YOU'RE A DRAGON

GAMEBOOK

SEVEN OF STARS

YOU'RE A DRAGON

GAMEBOOK

SEVEN OF STARS

Mae McKinnon

DRAGONQUILL PUBLISHING

Cover design by Marlene Ockersse
Formatting by Marlene Ockersse
DQ Logo by Juliane Voelker
WWFantasy Font by WindWalker64
Mael font by Dale Harris

First printed in France, 2018

ISBN 978-91-984558-2-3
A CIP catalogue record for this book is available from the National Library of Sweden

DragonQuill Publishing
www.dragonquillpublishing.wordpress.com

To Sherwin Tjia
You might never read this, but
Thank You
for rekindling my love of
gamebooks

This is a gamebook

If you are already familiar with gamebooks, create-your-own-adventures, pick-a-plots, or other solitaire adventures with branching paths, then just dive right into your new life as a dragon at **101** and see what wild adventures awaits you.

If this is the first time you hold a gamebook of any sort in your hand, then think of them as a book where YOU make the choices.
For every choice you make, the path you take through the story will branch, meaning you can read the book many times without getting the same ending or even without getting the same story.

Will you soar through the sky on heroic wings?
Will you burn the world with your evil flame?
Rescue the Princess?
Eat the Prince?

<u>How to Play</u>

- Begin your adventure at the section numbered **101** (on the next page).
- At the end of every section there are between one and four options, choose one and go to the numbered section indicated to continue the story.
- There are **over twenty different endings**. Which one will you get?

101

It's late. The streetlights are turning on as you walk down the cracked pavement. Just another few streets and you'll be home, you think. You've taken this route so many times before, you could probably walk it blindfolded if you had to. That's when you get the brilliant idea of taking a shortcut. Your family is cooking your favourite, it's your big day after all, and you'll be home sooner that way, right?

Turning into the alley you've always been avoiding, you're surprised by how bright it is, even when you've long since left the last of the comforting glow of the streetlights behind you.

It's a mighty strong lamp, you think as you shade your eyes. As you peer into the brightness, the warm light flickers, like lost flames. Except there is no fire. There's no lamp, either. It's moving … growing … almost as if it's alive.

Then, as the light grows even stronger, it pulls you physically forward. It envelops you, every part of you trying to be in two places at once. You black out.

You're woken up by the sharp scent of nature. Not the smells of the tame verges you're used to, this smells wild and free, with more than just a hint of the unknown.

Things are brighter than you remember them. The colours more intense. You blink, not sure how long you've been out for.

Gathering yourself together, you manage to rise on your elbows, giving you an unimpeded view of the soft, green grass you've been resting on; tall, willowy, grass that's never seen a lawnmower other than an herbivore's teeth.

Wait? Grass? Last you remember, there was asphalt under your new shoes and the stale smell of empty garbage bins in the summer.

Looking down, you jerk back. There's something large and scaly down there, on the ground! It's got *huge* talons. A monster! You try to stifle a scream, but all you can hear are deep rumbles. Trying to back away, slowly, your heart throbs heavily against your ribcage. But oh, no … the paw is moving too.

You quickly scrabble even further backwards. Away. You must get away! But the large, scaly, limbs follow you. You trip over a new set of feet and collapse in a heap.

The beast stops moving.

Carefully, you lie there trying not to move, to not provoke it, in case it'll attack. Nothing happens for several minutes. A horrible suspicion begins to form and, after a deep breath, you wiggle your little finger.

A scaly digit wiggles back.

No, not back. It's *you*. You're the one doing this.

After the first shock wears off, you examine yourself. Thank goodness. All arms and legs seems to be attached. Only, they're not exactly *your* arms and legs anymore. To start with, they bulge with muscles, and they're absolutely covered with scales. Not to mention, you seem to have grown extra appendages … wings even.

You are … in fact … a dragon.

If you want to go look for something to use as a mirror, so you can get a better look at yourself, turn to **105**

Adventure waits for no one, and you've got the best armour in the world now, so why worry? You decide to go exploring. Turn to **205**

102

The knight comes awake with a frightful clanging and a great deal of yelling variants of 'Begone foul beast!'

You nearly bite him in half, you're so offended, but a lot of stick figures drawn in the grass later (who knew dragon claws were capable of such artistry?) and the two of you reach an understanding.

'By Jove, a truce then,' he exclaims in a metallic voice.

You learn that his name is Sir Chopalot and he agrees to lead you to a young tree he knows of in return for you bringing him with you when you leave.

*Cat Companion: Chaos glowers at the new addition to your party through narrowed eyes. Turn to **162***

*Every step clanks and clonks until your ears are ringing. You can't understand why he doesn't just take off the armour. With it on, he's moving so slow that he might be a threat to snails but hardly anything else. Turn to **190***

103

The useless furball soon returns with an oddly shaped flower in its mouth. It's glowing with a gentle, golden light.

*You have no idea what it is, and it's way too small for you to handle, so you reluctantly let the cat bring it back to your growing hoard. Turn to **158***

104

You look and look, but you can't find Lightwing anywhere. Looks like this is one challenge where you're on your own.

*While you are otherwise occupied, the gryphons' numbers are dwindling. You better grab a rock, any rock, quickly — or you'll get left behind. Turn to **268***

105

You soon come across a shallow pond. It's a good thing there's barely any

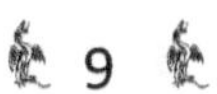

wind today. It means that you can use it as a mirror.

Looking down into it, something else stares back. You blink. It blinks back. There's a snout. A handsome, elongated face. Deep set, vibrant eyes that swirl with colours of amber and fire. Horns and spikes that would make even the most well-endowed porcupine jealous.

You blow out air from nostrils a small bird could get lost in. It sends ripples across the pond, distorting the image into a thousand reflections.

So, that's you, is it? You're not sure where you are or what happened, but you can recognize a dragon when you see one. Brilliant! You always wanted to be a dragon.

Holding your breath when looking back into the pond, you're careful not to disturb the surface this time.

So, what *do* you look like?

Majestic is a word that was invented just for you. Turn to **302**

Comparing yourself against the trees nearby, they're either very big trees or you're quite small, for a dragon. Turn to **114**

It's no wonder you startled when you first saw yourself. To be honest, you look a little scary. Turn to **255**

Wait, is that hair? Feathers? Turn to **145**

You're not sure you can define it, but you like *what you see. Turn to* **139**

106

Trying to hold your breath, you skim over a landscape filled with nothing but death and decay. Soldiers and weapons, battlebeasts, and torn standards litter the ground, forgotten by everyone except maggots and feasting crows.

Death isn't really your thing and with a mighty wingbeat you rise back into the sky. Turn to **310**

There are the sounds of battle still coming from further ahead. You decide to check it out. Turn to **256**

107

Wings flap open, catching in the increasing wind. A few leaps and bounces later and they're beating furiously to launch you into the sky.

The scents in this world might be confusing, but your eyes are sharper than ever. Scanning the forests and the plains, it's not long before you home in on your quarry. You spot a small group of deerlike creatures grazing in a glade. There's something else, about the same size, moving in the woods and … Jackpot! Out on the plains there's a whole herd of them.

Those look a little different, but they're still close enough for you to think of them as deer. Or maybe it's some sort of caribou?

The critters in the glade smell better to you, so you abandon interest in the herd. Slowly, you begin to circle. Tighter and tighter you turn, nothing more than a speck of dark against the suns. Then, you dive. Turn to **119**

The glade looks a bit small to you. You like feeling the open wind under your wings. Dipping gently to the left, you begin to climb. No sense in letting your prey know you're there until you're ready to strike. Turn to **346**

108

When something appears in the shadows, you're thrilled. Pulling yourself up, you try to look as threatening as possible. Every frill and spike showing at their most pointy.

The hulking shadow grows by the second and you're having second thoughts about this. Turn to **146**

Something stings your tail. Turn to **254**

109

Even as you're thinking the thoughts, the crystal simply just melts away before your eyes. It reveals a large, ornamental, gold bracelet inlaid with the largest rubies you could have imagined. And what did you know, it's a perfect fit for a dragon's forearm.

*You grunt your appreciation and, after admiring your new treasure, pat the ground where the crystal encasement once stood in gratitude. Turn to **156***

110

You spend a few hours in the morning chasing pigeons, scaring up flocks of the white and grey birds with your surprise moves. It sends an exhilarating rush through your body, from muzzle to the tip of your tail, swooping and diving like that.

Then, having had your fill of fun and food for a while, you remember what the Archmage said. Since you don't want to explode, you decide to head towards the first challenge. You do wish he could have given you a bit better guidance on what it's supposed to be, though. Quests are tough enough as it is.

Gryphon or cat companion: *Your companion nudges you from time to time as the two of you set out on your journey across the land. Looks like they know where you're going. You decide to follow their directions. Turn to **342***

*There are a lot of trees and hills where you are, but nothing that looks like the castle the Archmage told you to seek out for your first challenge, not even from the air. Looks like it's down to your best guess. Turn to **362***

111

The Castle of Stone doesn't like you attacking it, it seems, for it shudders. You manage to dodge the falling stones that, a moment ago, made up the parapet above you.

As the stones keep on falling (where are they all coming from?) you have no *choice but to abandon your rather precarious perch. As you glide away, the falling debris piles higher and higher until it covers the window. Turn to **387***

Gryphon companion:** Lightwing pecks you with her beak and shoos you away from the window. Turn to **180

112

'I fear that without stabilizing your condition, you will, eventually … ahem … explode.'

'EXPLODE?' you bellow.

The eruption from your throat is loud enough to startle you, and, sitting back down on your haunches, shuddering makes your scales rattle. Yikes. You don't want to suffer from premature exploditis.

'Just who are you?' you ask. 'How d'you know all this?'

'Me? I am Kaheiron. Archmage of the Twin Towers and I am, even if I say so myself, somewhat of an expert on dragons *and* magic.'

You grumble a bit but settle down and listen as the Archmage explains what you will need to do to avoid any exploding episodes.

Apparently, this requires several, hard-to-obtain ingredients. Why they can't simply keep them in stock, you don't understand, but apparently they need to be gathered by the person affected by the spell or they're less potent. And it undoubtedly requires *very* potent magic indeed to change a dragon into a human. Probably best not to risk it.

'No fear, young one,' Kaheiron says. 'Any such event is many months away. There will be plenty of time for adventure in between the challenges you'll face gathering the ingredients for this spell.'

You grin wolfishly. You like the sound of that.

Meanwhile, Kaheiron strokes his chin thoughtfully. 'It is a vast world out there and unknown to you. I've provided you with a list of what you need to gather but I am afraid I'm unable to accompany you myself. Still, perhaps you'd like a companion? And perhaps I could interest you in a map?'

You're curious what kind of companion he has in mind. A valiant knight? A *seeing-eye bug? A magic mirror? You must know. Turn to **369***

*A strong and proud dragon such as yourself have no need for companions. Besides, it'll be more fun to find your way on your own. Turn to **174***

113

There's a great milling about, but, oddly enough, you don't notice a single gryphon in the sky. They must be waiting for something. But what? And what has it got to do with you?

You try to flex a wing and accidentally knock into one of the many gryphons. This one, a male several shades darker in his leonine coat than many others here and with black points, gives you a steely eyed glare — a feat for which gryphons are well-equipped. Curling your lip at him, his tail swishes agitatedly. You hope you don't have to rely on him for anything in the future, because you're fairly certain you did *not* just make a new friend.

Then, one by one, the gryphons begin taking off. But they don't leave. Instead, they circle again and again until only you remain earthbound.

*With the lack of a translator, it takes a few swoops from one of the assembled gryphons before you realize you're meant to follow them. Turn to **199***

*Brow furrowing, you watch them for several minutes wondering what this all has to do with what you're supposed to fetch from Aawk Rock. Turn to **273***

114

Not that that doesn't make you far larger than any human, and a bit bigger than most horses, and that's not even counting your neck and tail, of which there are ample amounts. Not very good for sitting on towers and intimidating kings but excellent for getting through doorways.

Curling your tail experimentally, it slides over the grass, smooth as anything. You might be covered in scales, but they're hardly the gnarly type you'd have expected on a dragon, instead they're smooth and shiny. Taking a few steps, you're light on your feet, too. Bouncy even.

Isn't this exciting? You're a dragon *and* you can still fit through a door —
albeit it's going to have to be a very big door and you're going to have to
really suck it in, but you can do it.

Turning your small snout into the wind, you sniff a couple of times and sneeze.
Pollen. Evil pollen! There's something interesting ... over there. Maybe it's
worth checking out? Turn to **213**

Now, you just need to find out where you are. Maybe there's someone around
to ask? Preferably someone smaller than you. Turn to **205**

115

The next five minutes is nothing but a mad jumble of dashes, hot fire, even
hotter lava, and a lot of dodging. The coulee keeps striking at you. Its stamina
must be enormous. You doubt you can match it, but if you tire it out, maybe
it'll go back home and leave you alone?

Again and again you race around the rocky caldera, leaping from one uneven shelf to another. Parts of it are beginning to collapse. Where the coulee
strikes it, it's beginning to melt.

The young lavadragon, almost its whole body risen out of the boiling pool,
lunges at you. Again you dodge.

Looking over your shoulder, you slow down. Something's wrong. The
coulee isn't chasing you anymore. Instead it arches its broad back and lets out
a noise like an erupting volcano. Dark splotches are appearing on its fluid skin
— like cooling lava streams, spreading.

It's stayed too long away from its element. It's beginning to solidify, fast.
As the coulee lets out a keening sound, the crust envelops it. The coulee falls
against the caldera walls, its upper body shattering on impact.

One piece falls, bounces a few times off the rocks where it lands, before it
becomes nestled between two larger shelves.

It's amazing, you think, as you gaze into the fiery glow. It lives up to its name:
heart-of-fire. Still, it doesn't look much like a heart, more like a living rock,

but that's dwarves for you. You can return to them with your head held high. Turn to **304**

116

You can't wait to try out your new body and, after a few days of learning the ropes, or, the ways of the winds in this case, you get the hang of it. The next few months are one amazing adventure after another as you take in the sights, treasure, and the local cuisine in equal amounts — for who dares trifle in the affairs of a dragon?

Then, one day, after eating, cracks begin to appear in your armour. Glowing cracks within swirling fire.

You grow hotter and hotter until, a few days later, you explode.

117

You gleefully tear the palace apart. You might dent a claw or two in the process, but they're like fingernails, right? They'll grow back.

Eventually you locate the ruler's treasure. It's far more than you can carry in your paws, but there are some very fine rugs about. You tear a few down from the walls, pile on the larger items, and tie the ends together.

*You've never seen this much gold and jewels in your life. Certainly not in one place. The glimmer draws you in. You can't stop rifling through the treasure chamber for even better prizes. Turn to **163***

*Your crest knocks into a delicate looking tower close to the centre of the chamber, sending it crashing to the floor. No sense in tempting fate, you think, head swivelling to survey your new domain. Maybe you've done enough ... for one day? Turn to **264***

118

There are tufts of fur standing in every direction, but other than needing a good clean, the cat doesn't seem to be hurt by its ordeal. More like offended at having to be rescued.

It looks at you and meows imploringly, commandingly. For something so small, it sure has a lot of attitude, you think, and scoop it up. Standing there, in your paw, the cat looks into the wind, tail streaming, as if to say, 'What are we waiting for?'

You make a wide arc in the sky and head towards the plains in the distance. Turn to **342**

Onwards and upwards. Turn to **153**

119

The dive screams in your ears. Your wings quiver as you try to keep them steady. You're on course. Closer. Closer. Almost there.

The glade looks much smaller from up close. Much, much smaller. Too small.

You try to break in the air, flaring your sails, but you're too near to the ground. With a massive crunch, you knock into the trees at the other end of the glade, crashing through them as if they were matchsticks. Both you and the tree trunks become locked in combat, everyone and everything rolling over and over.

Next thing you know, your tail is buried under two massive trunks and your mouth full of leaves and the branches they're still attached to. You're also pretty sure you're upside down. Well, some parts of you, anyway.

Gryphon companion: *Lightwing squawks reproachfully at you. You don't need to speak gryphon to realize she's more than a little bemused by your actions. With her help, you're soon free of debris, though it takes a fair amount of nudging from her side to get you back into the air. Turn to* **167**

Looks like this is going to take a bit more practice. Even as a dragon, hunting takes skill. Especially if your prey is good at running away. Turn to **200**

120

Raking your claws and talons against the wall, you wonder if you can dig your way through the stone. Hitting it. Bashing it with your tail. Knocking against it with your horns (which only results in giving you a headache) — you try it all. But there doesn't seem to be any way in.

*In your frustration, you let out a roar that sends shivers through the very stone you stand on. The castle literally shudders and, as you let forth a fiery blast, it belches you out. You land in the lake with a mighty splash and when you turn back, the castle is gone. Turn to **387***

121

Beginning with a leisurely paddle, your swim soon becomes more adventurous. Turns out that when swimming as a dragon you're far more agile than when you were human and you take full advantage of this.

An explosion of air erupts as you breach, expelling what's left in your lungs in a mighty blow. Undulating through the water, you take another breath and disappear back down under the surface, only the plates on your spine showing as you speed out into the deeper parts of the lake.

*You can't feel the cold water through your scales and a mist is beginning to gather on the surface, so you dive deep down. Maybe there's an underwater entrance to the castle that you can use? Turn to **169***

*Something small and silvery flashes past you. You immediately give chase. Turn to **143***

122

For a while, you manage to dodge the coulee's attack. But you have to be lucky every single time, and the coulee only once. Its four not-quite-eyes watch your movements. Then, it strikes.

This time you don't manage to avoid it. Instead you're hit full-force by the entire might — and heat — of the young lavadragon. You barely have time to scream in anguish before your body turns to cinder.

123

Flying beneath clouds that are growing increasingly grey and billowing, you're caught in the crosswinds and, in a tumble, part company with the satchel that the Archmage gifted you.

Your companion gives a warbling call, folds her wings tight to their body like a falcon, and plummets after the disappearing satchel. You dive after them, stalling only when they pull out of their dive, wingtips brushing the water's surface, claws clasped firmly around their prey.

*Phew. That was lucky. Now you're really wondering what might be hiding in that unassuming satchel. It can't be just a leather bag, can it? Surely such a proud gryphon wouldn't have reacted so fast, had it been? Turn to **240***

*Once all bits and pieces, yourself included, are back where they should be, you set your eyes on the horizon and wonder just how far you can fly in one day? In one night? Turn to **200***

124

So close to your goal, you're not going to be swayed by any random excursion nor sidetracked by pretty glitter, no matter how much it glimmers like fools' gold.

*You fly straight and true. Turn to **270***

125

It takes no effort to glide out here. The heat from the desert spirals upwards. It sends you higher and higher until the whole of existence flicker before your eyes. You try to breathe, but there's barely any oxygen up here.

Adjusting your angle, you dive. Not the sharp dive of a falcon with prey in sight, but the powerful yet slow, descent of a condor. You keep having to shift your wings closer and closer to your body as the updraft is so strong it keeps trying to lift you higher.

From way up there, you catch sight of the first movement you've seen out here that wasn't shifting sand.

So, something is alive out here after all. You want to know what it is. Now! Turn to **311**

There's a flash of light in the corner of your eyes. Turn to **290**

126

Lapping at the water you've found, you spit it out, grimacing. The stream tastes foul. Like if someone had pulped death and blended it with honey and sugar. Raising your head high, continuing making, 'bleergh,' noises, you decide you don't trust this place. It looks harmless enough, but is it?

You're not planning on finding out the hard way, so with a bunch and a leap you return to the sky. At least that hasn't turned on you. Turn to **193**

127

From all your raidi— errr… travels, you've begun to amass quite the treasure trove. You've been keeping it close by, but when you get caught in a battle between thunderstorms, you get so tossed around that your already overflowing satchel breaks a seam. Unable to save all the preciousnesses, they tumble away from your grasp even as you try to snatch them out of the air. It's with an agonized cry that you scream vengeance upon the sky for stealing from you.

When the winds quiet down, you've been blown far. Farther than your wings would ever have carried you in a day under your own power. There are dry looking mountains wreathed in ochre and tinged red by the setting suns.

Beyond them you see nothing but sand, sand, and more sand. This must be the fabled Sandlands that you've heard about.

*It doesn't look very hospitable, but you've heard rumours that, deep in the Sandlands, there lies immense wealth for those strong enough to win it. And aren't you the strongest one of all? Of course you are. Turn to **332***

*Before you can even think about gathering more gold, you figure it's best to ensure that what you already have is safe. The mountains behind you look promising. You can probably find all sorts of caves in them. Turn to **305***

128

The four not-quite-eyes bore into you as you crouch on a shelf, ready to leap. Then, great eyelids, like slates of crags, slide over the coulee's eyes and it slowly sinks back under the surface. It has recognized you, a red dragon, as distant, *very distant*, kin.

*Phew, that was close. Too close. Turn to **313***

*Heaving yourself out of the caldera, you've had more than enough of this. Turn to **193***

129

The trail winds its way through the mountainous terrain. For a long time, the most interesting thing you see are some mountain goats. You track the trail through two more mountains, each one looking lusher than the last. You're moving away from the dryness of the Sandlands and back into a world of green forests and happy, bubbling little streams. Glah! How disgusting.

Then there rises before you another mountain. Larger than its brethren, even at this distance you can see that the whole top of the mountain has been sculpted, carved and incised, moulded in stone and metal until it stands as a giant fortress overlooking, well, everything.

Precious metal! Your eyes light up. This is more like it.

You have a vague memory of someone saying that attack is the best defence, so you do just that. Charge! Turn to **372**

Dwarves. It had to be dwarves. Still, it could be worse. Dwarven axes don't bite nearly as bad as a bit of elvish steel or, worse yet, a wizard's spell. Still, you decide to lay low until after dark. Turn to **395**

130

The landscape changes, becoming increasingly mountainous and rugged. The kind loved only by lost goats, some eagles, and … dragons. In fact, there are some up ahead. Riding the winds like majestic floating fortresses of scale and power to your eyes, the dragons you see are lithe creatures. Built for speed, not earth-shattering power.

You let out a mighty roar to let them know you're there. They're smaller than you. They should fall in behind you, follow your commands. It's all about who is stronger, right? Turn to **320**

You hover in the air as the others draw closer. They're looking mighty determined. A little too *determined. As they get closer and closer, you realize that they're not so small after all. Banking sharply, you dive to pick up speed. You're not up to facing other dragons. Not yet. Turn to* **275**

131

When you start swimming towards the castle, your companion races up and down the sad excuse for a beach, screeching at you. If you want to bring them with you to the Castle of Stone, you're going to have to give them a ride on your back, safely away from all that water.

Cat or Gryphon companion: *Bringing your companion forces you to swim,*

*Leaving your companion back on the beach, seething, as you strike out through the water in powerful moves, your strokes create a swell in your wake. It forces your companion to leap back when the small beach is drenched by the wave. Turn to **285***

*Nope. You don't like this idea at all. You gnaw angrily at your paw, give a mighty huff, throw out your head, and stalk off. Turn to **387***

132

Looking around, it doesn't seem like the village has a lot to offer someone like you and when you attempt to mime that you're hungry, everyone runs inside their homes and slams the doors.

*You decide to leave the good people alone. Obviously they don't know better. Turn to **160***

*Their lack of manners insult you. Don't they know better? Don't they know their betters when they see one? Your upper lip quivers as a growl begins to form at the back of your throat. Turn to **260***

133

When you get closer you see that there aren't any mushrooms after all. Just a collection of oddly mushroom-shaped rocks.

*You can't eat rocks, so shrug your massive shoulders and return to your journey. Turn to **342***

134

'So, you're not going to eat me then?' the princess asks, once she's settled down a bit. 'Dearhundt, there's a dragon in the garden. It promises not to eat us!'

You're a bit hurt at being called an "it." You're a dragon after all, not some mere bipedal cretin.

'If that's Seth, tell him to come back next week for the herbs he ordered,' booms a voice from within the cave.

'No, dear. This is a *different* dragon.'

'You sure?'

'I CAN tell the difference. And Seth is hard to miss, being all silvery. This is a *different* dragon!' she stresses, sounding exasperated, and rolls her eyes before she kindly invites you for tea … and cake.

*The tea you're not sure about, as you eye the china cups, but the cake sways it. Turn to **318***

*Shaking your behorned head carefully, you make a rumbling excuse about mistaken identities and leave. Turn to **279***

135

Before you manage to lift off, you're swarmed with kobolds gnawing and stabbing you wherever they can. They cling to your shoulders, around your horns, latch on to your tail and spikes. No matter how many you shake off, two more take their place. In the end, there is no escape.

136

The biggest rocks should be the highest, right? But, after a cursory flyover they're still too small for you. Then, you spot the perfect one, nearly down where the cliff meets the sea.

You get pelted by smaller debris from where the gryphons are furiously working to release their own choices from the iron grip of the stone, but ignore it, admiring the stone you pluck from the island of Aawk Rock. You didn't realize it would be quite this heavy, though, and it takes lots of huffing and puffing to get some good winds under your wings again.

*You've got your rock. Now, what possible use can you have for a large rock in the middle of the ocean? Turn to **268***

137

As you glide effortlessly on the winds, enjoying yourself, you spot something moving on a nearby mountaintop. It's a man.

At least, you presume it's a man. There's so much swirling, slightly grubby, cloth and bushy hair that it's a bit hard to tell, really. He's a very small man. But then, it's a very small mountain.

*You're not feeling up to talking to anyone, so you ignore the old man. Turn to **156***

*It looks mightily uncomfortable, sitting up there, but you're curious enough to circle for a while. You manage to land a bit further down and climb up to the strange mountaintop occupant. Turn to **191***

*Oh, look, lunch-to-go. Without slowing down, you sweep up the man in your jaws, do a slight toss and down your gullet he goes. Turn to **282***

138

You sleep.

And sleep.

And sleep.

Moss begins to grow on you. Flowers too. Beautiful flowers, all white and blue and sparkly, swaying gently in the morning breeze. With time, your body becomes just another hill in the valley amongst so many others.

139

You're the quintessential dragon. If someone wanted to *really* show someone, anyone, what a dragon really looks like, they'd be asking you to sit for a portrait.

You can't but help admire yourself in the cool reflection of the pond. If your scales could go, "zing" they would. Well, charisma is obviously not going to be a problem for you. Even your grin is magnificent, you think.

*Turning a snout the likes of which this world has never seen into the wind, you draw in several heavy scents. There's something interesting ... over there. Turn to **213***

*It's not really the most important thing, but, as you gaze around where you have landed, there is the small matter of where you are. Perhaps finding someone to ask would be prudent? Turn to **205***

140

You let out a mighty roar and shake your wings as deep horns are blaring across the stones — echoing between rocks and cliffs and metal helmets and armour.

There's a loud scraping noise, quick and sharp, and something swooshes through the air. You're hit by several tons of sharpened stone. It bats you to the side. As you struggle back on your feet, a stream of small bodies join the battle from hidden openings.

Outflanked — and by dwarves at that. Well, you'll soon see about that, is the last thought you have as the horde sets upon you with every weapon imaginable.

Hacked apart by small, walking armouries is not the most pleasant way to go and Death comes slowly.

141

The golden juices dribble down your chin. Their deliciousness permeates through your entire body, filling you with a kind of internal glow. You've never felt so well in your life.

'WHO DISTURBS MY GARDEN!?' suddenly booms out through the trees.

Your head jerks up guiltily. But, looking around you see no sign of the speaker. It had, however, been a very loud voice. Glancing down at the pile of branches and discarded pips at your feet, you wonder if maybe you shouldn't have eaten quite that many. As you do, the ground trembles. It sounds like footfalls. Giant footfalls. And they're coming closer.

Wait to see what's coming. Turn to **356**

Looking around furtively, you spy the best way to flee from the scene and dash away, tail streaming behind you. Turn to **303**

142

It's a tight squeeze — even more so than the mouth to the cave had been — but some grumbling and growling and wiggling later (is it your imagination or are your talons even larger and more curved than before?) and you manage to widen it enough. Turns out it opens up on a large set of caverns.

You're met with a glowing pair of slits. Eyes swirl dangerously at you. Whoops. Looks like this cave is already occupied — by a small wyvern no less.

Thinking that the wyvern might make an excellent guardian (and you don't even need to pay him) you look around for a place to hide your swag. Turn to **198**

Baring your fangs at your opponent, you expect it to back off. But it merely continues to hiss and spit in your direction, snapping its needle-sharp teeth trying to intimidate you. Turn to **228**

143

Snapping up a fish or two in passing, you roll through the teeming school, stunning several more with your tail. They bob around on the surface until your jaw snaps shut on them from beneath. Mmm … tasty fish.

*By the time you've outwitted, outsmarted, and outswum everything and everyone you can find, your limbs are aching after all that exertion. Turn to **383***

*The quest forgotten in the joy of discovery, you're having much too much fun to stop now. Turn to **277***

144

Putting your paw on the stone decanter, it zaps you with blue lightning. Trying again, the next shock is stronger. After another attempt, it's enough to numb your arm.

*That's it. This was a bad idea. You turn around and leave the way you came. Turn to **219***

*Maybe you'll have better luck with the crystal decanter? Turn to **267***

145

Nibbling gently at a raised wing confirms your suspicion. They're covered with large feathers and, as you part some with a talon, beneath them are soft downs. Perfect for stuffing a giant's pillow for the best night's sleep ever. Not quite what you imagined would cover a dragon.

You seem to be sleeker than you imagined a dragon to be, too — elongated even— and while you definitely have four feet, the front and back are spaced some distance apart, forcing you to curl your back like a lindworm in the sea. You seem to have acquired a thin moustache along the way — no wait, it's far too sensitive for that.

But you definitely have a beard and tufts on your ears. Long strands of thick, wavy, hair run down part of your neck, though the rest of your body is covered in pearlescent scales shimmering to every undulating move you make. How peculiar.

Turning your snout into the wind, you sniff a couple of times. Then your large ears pick up on it as well. Is it interesting? Maybe... Turn to **213**

You feel like you should already know, but the idea of finding someone to ask, just to confirm it, might be a good idea. Now, where would you find such a someone out here, in the middle of nowhere? Turn to **205**

146

Not long after, you come across the remains of a village. Landing with a heavy thud, you manage to get all your feet and tail down in working order, and crane your neck — a feat a dragon is particularly suited for.

It looks worse from down here. Where, from above, you could only see square and oblong patches of blackness, from down here there's all the rubble too. That and scattered remains of people's lives that somehow managed to escape the fire that destroyed this place.

There are a few dogs barking at the other side of what used to be a village, but they quickly run away when they notice you. Other than that, there doesn't seem to be anything here. No people. No animals, aside from a rat or two scurrying out of the way. No sheep. Nothing.

Well, almost nothing. There are small noises coming from below the rubble of one of the houses.

You roar at it to scare it up! Turn to **376**

Snort some flame into a likely looking hole, that'll light a fire under its tail alright. Turn to **293**

Leave well alone, you don't need this extra trouble. Turn to **153**

147

It's a bit awkward, but with the kobold acting as a translator, soon you're in a three-way conversation with the dwarves that appeared later, the actual masters of this mountain. You're kind of relieved, for the dwarves don't look at all pleased to see you. Supposedly having an armoured battle tank dropping in unannounced on your front porch can have that effect.

They frequently break into small huddles of hubbub from which mumbles of excited dwarfish well up.

Many hours later and you learn that they're willing to give you what you want, but, in return, they want you to lend them a hand — or a talon — or two.

Seems the greatest of Noame Mountain's forges has stood silent for centuries because no one has been able to re-ignite it. Being powered by dragonfire (back in the day dwarves and dragons must have had slightly more cordial relationships, you think), it's important enough to them that they're willing to overlook, grudgingly, everything so far.

*It doesn't sound too onerous, and you do need the trade. You agree to their terms. Turn to **402***

*Wouldn't the use of dragonfire mean you have to stay here and keep the forge going? Wouldn't that mean you can't complete the challenges or ever go home? That doesn't sound like a good idea to you. Turn to **230***

148

Curling up nose to tail you're soon snoring dragon snores. The reverberating sounds blasts out over the meadows in deep, thrumming booms. You continue to sleep and sleep and sleep.

The flowers, delicate and frail, reach up towards the sun, their gentle fragrance pooling at the bottom of the valley as the shadows grow longer.

Blotches begin to appear on your scales. Angry, purple blotches that grow by the hour and itch so much that even in your sleep your claws dig into your scales and hide, gouging huge wounds as you scratch and scratch at the itchy blotches and sores in your sleep, until there's not an inch of you that's not covered in purple and red.

You die there, surrounded by the pretty, but deadly, flowers.

149

You leap into the fray. Knocking aside buildings and toppling towers as the battle rages across the city streets.

But narrow (for a dragon) city streets and boulevards are no place for a draconic battle. The buildings, even the rubble from their remains, keep getting in the way. Especially the ones that are made to collapse on top of you.

*Tired and sore, you decide to vacant the premises post-haste. Turn to **380***

*It looks like your enemies have brought in new blood. It smells strange, even through all the dust and smoke. Looks like you're going to have to fight your way out of this one. Turn to **312***

150

You flee the garden. Some battles just aren't worth fighting. The golden fruit didn't just taste delicious, it took the choice as to whether or not you should return to your world right out of your hands. You discover that you will no longer be able to return to human form and will now have to learn the ways of this new world. You will also no longer explode, the Archmage explains once the two of you meet again.

What will you make of your new life as a dragon? Well, that destiny now rests entirely in your own paws.

151

The dwarves aren't too happy when you return without the reagent you'd promised them. But they're willing to give you another chance. Somewhat scornfully they suggest that perhaps the lesser reagent will be a more appropriate challenge for you.

You turn them down, quite impolitely as they annoyed you with suggesting you were less than capable. Turn to **193**

Such insults from such an inferior species! How dare they? Attack! Turn to **296**

It bites and gnaws at your heart, but you agree to make an attempt at the other reagent. Turn to **222**

152

You blink and the sparkle is gone. No, wait. There it is again. You shoulder aside a few beech trees and there it is. A wood-pool.

Arching your neck proudly to see better, the waters from up here alternatingly look pitch black and crystal clear. How odd.

And is that something at the bottom? You're not sure if it's a statue or just some glimmering, rusty old sword. But rust doesn't glimmer, does it?

For a moment, you wonder if you should maybe grab a tree trunk or something but, in the end, you figure your claws are much better at fishing out whatever glimmers at the bottom of the pond. Turn to **319**

Oh, no, you've seen this movie. This is a bad idea. A bad idea, you tell yourself. Still, your instincts tingle at the sight. Turn to **384**

153

For a while, there is nothing to distract you but cotton clouds billowing and flowing around you as you swoop through an ever changing landscape of milky white. Exhilarating at first, it soon grows mundane and all the jigging and zigging and sharp banks are making your wings ache. You might have plenty of wing muscles, but they're not used to actually being *used*.

Then, through a break in the clouds, you spot shapes moving across the ground far below.

You probably wouldn't have noticed if it was only one, but the dusty plains are fairly teeming with them — like scurrying ants on a very flat anthill.

You begin gliding downwards for a better look. Turn to **339**

There are some interesting dark specks on the horizon, too. Are they dragons ... or something else? Turn to **310**

154

Keeping your distance, you circle the castle again. It doesn't look any more inviting the second time. There is lichen growing on the outer walls. Drips of water (stale by the smell of it) trickles down from above, and the dark window slits sit there like empty, soulless eyes.

It looks like one of those places that rises from the deep only one night every hundred years, during the full moon, claims the life of some passing adventurer foolish enough to enter, and then vanishes again, leaving only an unpleasant aroma in its wake.

Roaring defiantly, you claw in the air as if there was a physical barrier. But no matter how many times you circle the castle, the result is the same. Turn to **367**

Maybe if you climb really high and then dive straight down you can break through the barrier? Turn to **173**

155

You wake up to someone prodding you with a stick.

'Dearhundt,' the pleasant voice calls loudly. 'You've got a dragon in your garden ... again.'

Opening a large eye, you discover that the stick is actually a broom, and the one swinging it must be the princess — though she doesn't look anything like any princess you're familiar with. For starters, she's not wearing a crown, not even a diadem set with pearls. Instead, her hair is tied back with a ponytail and over her dress she's wearing a leather apron. It has painted flowers on it.

'Shoo! Shoo!'

The princess pokes you with the broom again. You must have caught her in the middle of cleaning, for the bristles are full of cobwebs and dust.

*The way she's waving that thing around, she's going to hurt someone, you think. Turn to **326***

*Backing down, you try to make yourself as small and non-threatening as possible. You draw the line at pretending to be a dog though, all four feet in the air, hoping for a tummy rub. Turn to **134***

156

There has to be more interesting things around here. Question is, what? You strain your keen draconic eyes to see across the lands beneath you, searching. Always searching.

So, in what direction will you turn your majestic self now?

*This way looks interesting. It has mushrooms. You remember about the mushrooms. Turn to **133***

*No, you'd much rather spin fast and then head in whatever direction your snout points when you, somewhat dizzy, stop. Turn to **221***

157

Pushing aside the underbrush and trees alike, what once was a path leads you to a hole into the ground. It's dark, as holes tend to be, and you'd be quite curious about it if it didn't assault your nostrils with a stench worse than rotten mackerel.

There are a few, rusted through, weapons scattered around it, but when you try to pick one up it disintegrates in your paw. You're not going to find anything useful here by the looks of it.

Best to get out from below all these trees and get a dragon's true perspective on this new world, you decide. Turn to **137**

A bit of walking later — a dragon covers a great deal more distance than a human, so you get pretty far from the hole — your ears twitch. Something's out there. Turn to **362**

158

Wonder which tunnel you should choose this time — or maybe you should go back and check on one you've already been in?

You head down the first tunnel. Turn to **286**
You'll chance the second tunnel. Turn to **322**
It's tunnel number three for you. Turn to **338**

159

As your hind legs stretch out, talons questing for the white orb going up and down on the waves, up and down, your wingtips splash into the water, making you lose your balance. A shadow in the water shoots upwards. Algae-encrusted teeth as big as your head bite into your left wing, rending it asunder.

You flap uselessly as the anglerfish monster tosses its head, churning the ocean into a cauldron of white foam specked with red. Caught in the enormous maw, your cries echo over the empty ocean before you're dragged into the dark depths of the trench below.

160

As you leave the village behind, you at least manage to scrounge up some rabbits. Better than nothing, but there's nothing else for it, you're going to have to start of this whole adventure on less than a full stomach.

Things could be worse, you think. Something might have tried to eat you instead. Turn to **200**

161

There are fields of wild flowers and tufty barley grass for you to enjoy. Best of all, there doesn't seem to be anyone other than you and, well, nothing. Peace and quiet at last.

*The scent from the flowers is quite nice. Going for a roll in them should wash the fire and soot from the forge away. Turn to **288***

*You're thirsty. The small stream nearby should quench it nicely. Turn to **126***

162

Sir Chopalot moves so slowly, you wonder what good all that armour does him without a horse to carry him, and you eventually relent and let him climb aboard. At least this way you'll get there *before* sunset.

It's a tactic your feline companion responds to with hisses and yowls. That was Chaos' favourite spot!

*Retreating up your back, nestled amongst your swaying plates, the grey cat stares daggers at the knight. Turn to **190***

163

The sound of gold fills your ears. You didn't realize it was so pleasing, so soothing. It's not cold at all, but warm and filled with the promise of more. Pick me. Pick me. It all seems to call out. You dig into the pile you created when tossing all those chests, scattering their innards of precious stones and metal, with talons and paws. It even feels good against your scales.

But what is this? Something stings your rump. Your behorned head jerks up, knocking another hole in the roof. Growling, you shuffle around, only for something to sting you right between your nostrils.

You've lingered too long. The valiant defenders of the city have rallied reinforcements. And these aren't your run-of-the-mill mercenaries either, you realize as a stronger "zing" almost penetrates your breastplate.

They're using magic.

That's not fair.

*Letting out a loud hiss, you gather yourself for what is to come. To battle then! Turn to **312***

*What do they take you for? A fool? They're bound to have other weapons that might "really" hurt you. Best to make yourself scarce. You can always come back later to exact vengeance. Turn to **264***

164

There's a flash of light, then another. It's coming from below you.

*Circling wide, eyes peeled, you scan the waves from high above. Turn to **272***

*Veering off, you make a shallow dive towards the ocean's surface. Turn to **385***

*You carefully lower yourself with powerful wingbeats until you nearly stand still over the water. Turn to **371***

165

Sauntering into the filled chamber as if he owned it, Chaos' tail brushes against several of the diamond-studded goblets as he passes them. You watch as the cat pads up to a rather disappointing chalice — there's not a single precious stone adorning it — and jumps up on top of it.

You rumble something insulting, curling a long digit in his direction. Chaos throws you a glance then proceeds to wash his face.

*Once he's sure of your attention, Chaos bats at the chalice until it falls over, then chases it all over the floor, until you manage to hook it at the very point of a talon. That's one challenge down. Turn to **340***

*Putting the chalice away, you wonder where you should head next. Maybe you should try going north? Turn to **401***

166

It feels like forever before it's your turn, but it's hardly any time at all. Then you too fold your wings and dive. You can feel the air burning against you. It tears at your body. Tries to squash your eyeballs down into your tail. Yet you still go faster.

The ground is coming up at speed. You roll hard, swinging around and, without being quite sure how you got there, for a moment, you fly wingtip to cliff off Aawk Rock.

The coastline here is much more rugged than you imagined from the air. Outside of the actual land, rises pillars of stone where the sea has eroded away the cliff and is slowly winning the battle of supremacy. The cliff isn't giving up without a fight, though. Uneven, broken, yet proud, the stone pillars strive towards the sky.

Some are larger, thicker. Others thinner. Others yet curl like bridges. Through all of them the gryphons are swerving and jinking, sometimes so close that the tip of their wing feathers brush against the crumbling rock.

It seems they're competing in who can pass by the pillar without getting knocked into the sea. You hope you're not going to have to keep this up all around the island. This is probably a futile hope.

Up ahead there is a pillar grander than the rest. Rushing towards it, you can make out that everyone is climbing up, rolling and then diving through a hole carved into its middle.

*Oh, no! You won't fit. Pull up. Pull up. Turn to **378***

*Dive through the hole in the rock. Turn to **317***

167

Once you're back in the sky where you belong, albeit a little unsteady — guess dragons aren't quite as shock-absorbent as you thought they were — Lightwing circles around you for a while.

Then there's a high, trilling call, and you get to watch as your companion rolls, tucks their wings tight against themselves, and plummets towards the earth like an avenging peregrine. She's spotted something.

Swooping in, the gryphon expertly trusses up one of the running deer-caribou, tossing it into the air like a playful kitten. It bleats, eyes rolling, but before it can crash to the ground, the gryphon catches it again.

*Though you're feeling just a touch resentful at how effortless Lightwing made the manoeuvre seem, both of you eat well that night. Turn to **246***

168

The cat is gone before you even have time to blink. Your feline companion makes another amused sound, which you could have sworn was cat for, 'What did you expect, you *are* a dragon!'

*Throwing yourself back into the air, you head for the faint mountains in the distance. Turn to **209***

*Tally Ho! Turn to **153***

169

It's a good thing dragons can hold their breath for a really long time because the lake turns out to be much deeper than you anticipated. For a while, it grows darker and darker as you move away from the light filtering down.

Careful not to choke on it, you taste it with your tongue. Yuck, it even *tastes* murky.

*The water is beginning to feel cold against your scales. It didn't do that before. Should you turn back? Turn to **374***

Reorienting yourself in the direction you think the castle is, you decide to go looking for that underwater entrance. All castles and fortresses and their ilk next to the water has them, don't they? Those handy tunnels and pipes *leading straight to the heart of the matter with only an iron gate or two blocking the way. Turn to **280***

*Feeling uneasy about this whole thing, you look around for another path. Turn to **393***

170

You head down the large passage with a swagger then, just around the first bend, it stops. You're going to have to back up.

*Deciding that you've had enough of caves, maybe trails are more interesting. Particularly ones that try to hide from you. Turn to **129***

171

The slopes of the volcano are practically devoid of anything resembling plant life. The only thing you see are the scattered remains of what might have been trees, once upon a time; the snags for which Mt Snag must be named, you guess.

It's a good thing your paws are sturdy though, for every step you take you never even notice the heat beneath your feet, or the formations that would have torn human feet to shreds.

Several hours of combing it, sniffing it (and sneezing fireballs as a result), as well as digging a few holes, just in case what you're looking for is hiding beneath the surface, the only thing you've found is boredom.

*There's really something working against you. You can feel it. In your very bones you can feel it. Turn to **151***

*There are some darker patches on the south side of the volcano. You decide to try there first. Turn to **390***

172

Cutting your adventure short, you travel swiftly enough, driven by agitation as much as powerful wingbeats. As a result, you arrive at the meeting place early. There's no one there.

*That's some nerve, you think. There isn't even anyone here. Well, if they think you're going to just sit around and wait for them, they don't know you. Turn to **331***

*It looks like there's nothing to do but wait. You hate waiting. Turn to **291***

173

It's hard work and you're soon getting short of breath. When it feels like you just can't climb any higher, you push yourself just a little more, then roll and tuck your wings close to your body. The wind screams in your ears. The speed is unbelievable. Down. Down, you go.

As you pass through the outer layers protecting the castle, spasms race through your body. Curling up in the air in pain, you're suddenly spinning out of control.

*Your stomach heaves and your insides turn to knotted jelly. Then your body takes over and, shivering from the experience, you manage to get away from the castle's influence. You're not trying that again. That's no way forwards. Go back to **154***

174

You can't imagine why you'd want to be saddled with a companion. There's a whole world out there to explore and the last thing you need is someone around that keeps telling you what you can't do.

*Now, where should you go first? Turn to **200***

175

You're hungry enough that when you come upon a patch of bushes heavy with black, oval berries, you don't just sniff them experimentally, you snap up half a bush in your jaws, spitting it out again just as quickly.

Bleh! Sour and acidic, the berries aren't ripe and the leaves taste even worse.

*Follow the path to the right. It's got to lead somewhere, right? Turn to **157***

*There's an overgrown path to your right, but why follow it on foot when you can fly? Turn to **137***

176

There's no trouble at all for someone as strong as you to push the stone lids off. Looks like the residents have been dead for quite some time. The wrappings around the bodies have become loose and might have been partially eaten by mice — though how mice might have gotten in to the stone coffins in the first place you don't know. Maybe they have mice here that eat rock?

Their work has left several of the valuables these people were buried with exposed and, grinning, you make short work of the rest.

Now you've got several shields, beakers, and jewel-encrusted swords to add to your growing hoard.

*You return to the main cave with your new treasures. Turn to **158***

177

Deciding that the shortest route isn't the most fun, finding an alternate one, on this map that you have, is going to make this flight a little tricky. If only you weren't up against Father Time.

*This could be one long detour if you're unlucky. Turn to **323***

178

It's not easy, but by holding your breath and making yourself as small and thin as possible, you manage to squeeze in between thick, wiry trunks of brown and grey. The bark is so rough that you scrape off a few scales in the process.

You search for hours but the soft green and orange — so light it was almost yellow — is nowhere in sight. Either it's much further away than you thought or it was all just a trick of the light.

*But wait, something glimmers in the moss up ahead. Turn to **214***

*Thinking it'll be too tight a squeeze, you circle back until you reach the outskirts of the forest again, your scales full of pinelike needles that itch something terrible. Turn to **215***

179

Walking is a bit cumbersome, but you soon hit your stride and it does give you ample time to get used to your new body. By nightfall, you actually feel quite comfortable with it. Your wings you stretch periodically, just to feel that they're there. It's only your tail that still causes you trouble. You and everything it crashes into when it twitches and sways — almost as if it has a mind of its own.

*Thankfully, your draconic strides are wide, carrying you far, before night begins to creep in. Turn to **240***

*Twilight eventually descends, but you're not the least bit tired. It feels like you could do this for ages. Why stop now? Paws churn the earth and you decide to just keep walking through the night. Turn to **200***

180

Judging by the size of the opening, you don't think there's any chance that

Lightwing will fit through it, but the gryphon squawks impatiently at you, and, hanging from the heavy stones of the windowsill, manages, to your surprise, to flow through it without barely losing a feather.

After that, actually retrieving the chalice is easy, her claws clicking on the cold floor as she saunters over and carefully picks it up with a taloned foot.

*Looking rather smug, upon her return, Lightwing deposits the chalice in your satchel. Turn to **340***

181

You barely feel the weight of the traveller as he settles down amongst your spines and platings, wriggling about a bit to avoid the more knobbly ends.

Turns out he was searching for lute strings and, by the time you reach the inn, The Broken Beaker, he's been talking your ear off *and* restrung it. Obviously he must have found some, though how you'd find lute strings on a volcano is a mystery to you.

The inn only caters for beings up to a certain size and you exceed that by far, so you have to settle for curling up around the building, sticking part of your snout through the backdoor, and listening to the music and tales told by the other occupants: from adventurers, merchants, wandering elves, tinkers, bards, rogues, and quite possibly a thief or two (though no one is foolish enough to try to lift something from you. You wish they'd tried. It would have been fun to chase them).

*In the morning, once your head stops throbbing (that ale must have other things than just apples in it). You're unexpectedly offered a heart-of-fire as thanks by the traveller. Both for enjoying the music and helping out. A good deed, indeed. Now you can return to the dwarves with your head held high. Turn to **304***

182

You eventually come upon a hamlet consisting of little more than a few houses clustering together for protection amongst crops, fields, and pastures.

The fields don't look anything like what you're used to. Rather than billowing row upon row of golden wheat and corn, the plots are small and the plants scrawny. Equally scrawny are the cows and goats that lumber away from their grazing when they spot you.

When he sees you, the farmer tilling the nearest field stares at you for a full minute then shrugs and goes back to his work — though the two oxen pulling the plough are a lot unhappier about your presence, making a great deal of noise … and smell.

As you approach, it seems the few settlers aren't absolutely terrified of you, but they make known, in no uncertain terms, that they'd prefer you to leave.

You try to look less intimidating (not an easy task when you're saddled with so much history as a firebreathing menace) and give communicating one last shot. Turn to **132**

How dare they? You whip around, knocking over a small shed with your tail. You want food and you want it now. If they're not going to bring any, you're going to have to make your own arrangements. Turn to **260**

183

Soon after, the smell of roast fish overwhelms the entire island. Seems not just your group, but the others returning, are also invited to the feast. At first, everyone is responsible for cooking their own piece of fish (though where the fire came from is a complete mystery) but that seems to be the end of the ritual. After that, fetching more fish is left to a small group of younger gryphons who spend much of the coming evening flying back and forth between the festivities and the fresh supply of monster fish.

Sighing contently, your tummy round and happy, you doze, watching the gryphons gambol and dance. Something of their happiness is contagious, but all you have energy for is thumping your tail to the rhythm and a slight grin now and then.

Partway through the evening, your companion, prancing as giddy as a fledgling, comes over, dropping a small bundle of freshly picked herbs at your paws. Your reward for a challenge well won.

*Looking down at the offering you realize that the time has come. Time to see the wizard, or Archmage as he calls himself, you huff ... again. Turn to **360***

*Time is running short, but you're not quite ready to go home yet. Surely there's time for just one more, small adventure? Turn to **375***

184

It looks like something's living in here, you think. And not just the wyvern either. Soon though it becomes clear why you didn't see much trace of the comings and goings at the external cave mouth. There's a whole family of rodents living in here. Large ones too.

*You eagerly give chase when the furballs scamper away as you approach. Turn to **188***

*Nothing to see here. There's nothing else for it. You'll have to explore more. Turn to **158***

185

The formation skirts the coastline, close enough to the thundering waves that some of the spray lands on you like white foam. It's a struggle flying this close to the sea and you're grateful when the lead gryphon calls out a shrill challenge and suddenly banks sharply — straight into the cliff.

No, wait, there's a narrow gorge cutting into the island. That's where they disappeared into. One by one the gryphons in the formation follow them.

You turn the corner and the world, all of a sudden, looks to you like a giant battle of gryphon versus mountain. Raking their claws and talons against the cliffside, wings beating furiously to keep them in place, a shower of smaller debris strikes the gravelly beach below.

Then a dark gryphon, so dark the black tufts on their ears almost disappear in the rest of the fluff, flies past you carrying a chunk of rock. They're heading out towards sea again, slowly now.

You're bigger than any gryphon present, whatever is going on, you're getting yourself the biggest rock you can get. Turn to **136**

Gryphon companion: *You look around for your companion, Lightwing, but there are so many gryphons here, of all shapes and sizes and everyone seems intent on reducing the cliff to rubble. You can't see them. Turn to* **104**

186

There's no such thing as a comfortable interdimensional journey and once you wake up, back home, you're still seeing spots of light dancing before your eyes. You roll out of your bed, landing on the floor with a heavy thud and your legs entangled in your duvet.

Head spinning, you begin to pat yourself down, making sure all arms and legs are attached. Ah, good. They all seem to be there. Guess it must all have been just a really intense dream, you decide. Though it had felt so real. You also don't remember how you got home last night. You grab a shirt from where it's hanging over a chair and start pulling it over your head when you hear a noise.

Was that a meow just now? Turn to **345**

Did a low chirrup come from beneath the window? Turn to **373**

187

Clearing away the dust and cobwebs, you can now see the contents is some sort of red wine. Or what looks like red wine. You shrug. It can't hurt, can it? Just a tiny, little sip can't hurt a big, strong dragon like you, right?

Taking a hefty swig, you're almost hit by the glass bottle as it falls to the floor. It's become the size of a house.

No. Wait. It hasn't.

You've shrunk. A lot!

Thank goodness you still have wings, you think and start zooming about the chambers.

*Meaning to find a "grow" potion to reverse your not-so-good fortune, you instead zoom right out a window. Turn to **219***

188

Great. You needed that snack.

*Now you better find out where that trail outside leads. Turn to **129***

189

Most ordinary dragons, you included, aren't actually impervious to the molten innards of any world. Humans would have burnt to a crisp instantly. Your scales protect you for a moment before the heat drives through scales and flesh and muscles. The dying screams of a dragon echoes between the rock-walls long after the lava lake has swallowed your bones.

190

With your strides and the knight's helpful guidance, it's not long before you reach what you're looking for. But rather than a verdant tree, you're greeted with rumbles and loud hisses.

Yikes! The knight forgot to mention the sinuous beast wrapped around the tree you're wanting like a large, scaly sofa cover.

And look, there's a sword sticking out of the tree. If it could penetrate this kind of tree, you'd hate to see what it'd do to your scales.

*The young wyrm lifts its head and begins to sway slowly from side to side, cold, reptilian eyes watching your every move. Turn to **232***

Uh, no. You're not fighting that! Those fangs are practically dripping with *venom. This thing looks like a dragon killer. Turn to **284***

191

Grumbling something about loose rocks sink dragons as you carefully pick your way up the brittle and rock-strewn mountain, you can't help but startle when the greybeard turns to you and says, 'Greetings dragon. What brings you to my mountain? Please do not upset the boulders of wisdom.'

You rumble and whuff and the old man nods sagely, stroking his beard.

'I see,' he says, eventually. 'The closest city — the great city of Zuri — is several wings from here I fear, even for such a magnificent dragon as yourself. Hmm … maybe … no, I should not.'

You shouldn't what? You want to know.

'Perhaps I can, in my infinite wisdom, furnish you with the knowledge of somewhat of a shortcut?'

'Great!'

'For a price—'

Grrrr. Aren't sages supposed to have shunned worldly goods or something? You're sure you read that somewhere.

'Do you want my advice or not, dragon?'

*You agree that you do. No one said you had to follow it, after all. Turn to **295***

*Shaking your behorned crest, as you turn, your wings unfurl and you make an effortless leap off the mountain. Turn to **156***

192

The air around you begins to shimmer. Trying to follow the swirling patterns of light makes you dizzy, so you squeeze your eyes shut. The next you know you land on the ground with an, 'oomph!'

Ouch, you landed right on a rock … and there's another rock … You try to sit up using appendages you don't have and end up falling over again. This time you decide to take it slowly and, by chance, look down.

'Where the *** are my clothes?'

'Dragons are not in the habit of wearing clothes,' the Archmage says and offers you a one-size-fits-all tunic and some boots that are far too large for you. 'You've been a dragon for quite some time.'

You snatch the clothes from his hands and dress hurriedly. Hopefully there will be some better clothes in your future because these are definitely not comfortable.

'There will be much for you to learn, but perhaps first we should see about returning to the Towers.'

The Archmage snaps his fingers. You look around expectantly, but rather than an instant change in scenery after a burst of magic, all you see are several people — dressed for the great outdoors and with an assortment of smaller weapons strapped on — dash forward from below.

Kaheiron, who you now realize is actually both quite tall and slender and dressed in magnificent embroided robes accented with purple, offers you a small smile.

'Magic never is quite what people expect,' he says. 'Nor are dragons, for that matter. Remember that when next you meet one in human guise.'

193

Soaring in the sky is exhilarating at the best of times and what worries you have just seems to melt away and peel off, stolen by the wind before you know it. The mountains stand tall and proud, capped with snow and ice practically glowing in the sunlight.

From up here the world looks so peaceful, a mix of green and blue and brown and ochre. And white, of course — and not just the thin veil of clouds that you burst through whenever dipping below to see the sights, either.

After that exhilarating flight you're in a good mood. A mood that dissipates quickly when you realize that you're not entirely sure where your third challenge is located. Turn to **177**

You'll have to land again if you want to check your map, assuming you still *have it. Turn to **203***

Gryphon companion: *Lightwing trills. It sounds like a songbird, only a hundred times louder, and you've learnt that it's the gryphon form of laughter. You're not the only one that finds flying this free exhilarating.* *Turn to **399***

194

Before you even reach landing distance, you're met with a swarm of squawking, warbling gryphons. Their eyes have seen everything and they drive you off with talons and claws and beaks, pecking and slashing at you until you turn back towards the mainland.

Looks like you'll have to join up with the Archmage without *all the pieces he asked you to gather.* *Turn to **172***

195

The cat runs you over with its eyes, while pretending to watch something more interesting, in the corner, over there, by the willows. How typical, you think. You're a mighty, fearsome beast of unimaginable power but the cats of *any* world are *still* not impressed.

Then, with a small huff, it saunters over and, claws scraping against your scales for purchase, it climbs onto your back and sits down on your shoulders, draping its long, luxurious tail over its feet.

Turning your head (a manoeuvre you'd never have dared if you had still been human), your eyes narrow as you watch it. It's quite a handsome cat, with well-groomed fur and dark, swirling markings in its otherwise steel grey coat. It looks back at you, as if to say, 'Why aren't we moving already?'

'Hey, wasn't I the one that was supposed to choose?'

Kaheiron merely smiles graciously. 'His name is Chaos. Remember, we cannot return you to your world until the spell has stabilized and run its course,' the Archmage calls out as you head off.

You think he makes it sound like you've caught the sniffles or something.

You figure you should spend some time learning to use your wings properly, *so your talons dig into the soft earth as you start your journey — on foot. Turn to **179***

*It's harder than you anticipated to get airborne, but you manage. Now, flight quickly carries you away from the Twin Towers. Turn to **316***

196

Your scales, safe for the moment, shudder. You decide to try your luck further away. But with all the blood pumping through your veins, every direction looks the same.

*Gryphon companion: Lightwing nips you sharply on the shoulder with her beak. Her bright eyes cloud over as you turn around and pick up speed, but she follows you, for now. Turn to **239***

*You have no idea where this direction will take you, but at least it's away from here. Turn to **337***

197

Something, you don't know what, rouses you from your deep sleep. As you wake, you realize that you're itching something terrible. Glancing down at your forearm, it's covered in small, purple blotches — like if they'd been stained by ink.

Your scales feel loose, like one of those bad dreams where your teeth threaten to fall out, and your muscles ache with every motion. Struggling to your feet, you take a deep breath and sneeze violently.

Still woozy and weak, you tighten your haunches and leap back into the sky with a mighty shove and pumping of wings.

*You're hoping that you'll find a large lake somewhere. You desperately need to wash off and soothe your itching scales. Turn to **193***

198

Stashing it near the wall, rasping your talons across the rock to bury it under some debris, you try to work quickly, and back away the way you came before the wyvern gets any ideas. It hisses at you the whole time.

*Job done, you return outside. Best to investigate that faint trail just in case there are heroes or thieves about. Turn to **129***

199

Taking off to join everyone, you're a lot bigger than they are. You just have to hope none of this is going to involve very tight-fitting spaces.

The airborne ball of gryphons (and one dragon sticking out like a watermelon amongst ripe cherries) circles tighter and tighter, spinning. Then the spinning ball of fur, feathers, and scales suddenly splits in two. You only have moments to decide which to follow.

*Follow the group that is climbing. Turn to **245***

*Fold your wings and try to catch up with the group that's diving towards the coastline. Turn to **185***

200

After a night's sleep, your stomach rumbles loudly, reminding you that you didn't get anything to eat. You shake your head. No. Negative thought. Don't all great heroes suffer hardships on their journeys? Surely, a little hunger isn't going to stop you?

Grinning widely, you raise your head proudly. What's a missed dinner or two when there's adventure to be had?

Flexing your muscles, you admire their supple motion beneath your scales. Scraping your claws against a nearby rock formation, you're sure no one will doubt who passed through here now. Turn to **175**

201

The dwarves aren't too happy when you return without the reagent you'd promised them. How a strong dragon like you could have failed at acquiring some mere pieces of wood, that's something they refuse to believe, thinking instead that you never even made the attempt in the first place.

Despite you offering to go after the other reagent instead, they now consider you to have renegaded on your deal and they return to their city in the mountain, closing the doors and leaving you alone out amongst the stone huts and fields.

Hunching your shoulders, you put your weight on your hind legs and launch yourself at the door. Turn to **296**

Head and tail drooping, you admit defeat on the second challenge. Maybe you'll have better luck with the last one? Turn to **193**

202

The storm tosses you around for a few hours before you manage to defeat it. Dragons aren't meant to spin as if they've been tossed into the washing machine of heaven, you think, as you strain to find a safe place to land. You really need to dry out your wings. You'd swear the rain has penetrated them to the bone.

Only too late do you realize that the spot you so carefully scouted isn't empty.

'Nothing good will be achieved by this path that you have chosen,' the dark-haired Archmage intones dramatically.

He'd look quite good with a few flashes of lightning behind him, you think. You shake your head, trying to dislodge that thought. No. Mustn't let him trick you.

'I can help you,' the Archmage calls after you as, in a flurry of dust and mud,

you return to the sky. Turn to **392**

Gryphon or cat companion: *The wizard/mage/sorcerer or whatever he wants to call himself is clearly trying to con you. Hah! You know that scam. You're not going to fall for it. Your companion, it screeches at you, trying to make you turn back. Turn to* **237**

203

Landing heavily on a deserted looking outcropping, you carefully unfold the map and heave a heavy sigh (and when dragons sigh, it's not a small endeavour). There's a small dot far out to sea. That's where you're going. Far, far out to sea.

Turn seawards. Turn to **323**

204

Peering over the edge, not even your eyes manage to penetrate the veil that obscures the bottom. If there *is* a bottom. Sulphur and other gases waft up from the enormous shaft. You kick in a small rock, listening for when it hits something hard. Nothing happens. It's like it evaporated.

Beginning the climb down, your talons leave huge gashes in the rocks, and with the steep and uneven surface, you're glad you're a dragon and not some human explorer. They'd probably have been cooked before they even got forty metres down.

The smell is worse than anything you've ever smelled before. Like a mix of fermenting seaweed and rotten eggs. Bleh. If you're going to hunt for the reagent in the caldera, you decide you'd better do it quick. Turn to **308**

It really does stink down here, and the smell burns your nostrils. You turn around and start to climb back up. Turn to **313**

Choosing to do your first bit of exploring by foot, you set off. You've always wondered what it'd be like as a dragon in a faraway world. What are you? What will you become? Can you speak? You run a large tongue over enamelled points. It'd be convenient if you could speak. You then try out a few phrases.

'Cat. Hat. Sat in a lap.'

The words make perfect sense in your head, so obviously you still think in your normal tongue, but all your ears are hearing is 'Rumble, rumble, growl.'

'Maybe another dragon could understand me? But, I can't even understand myself. Bugger!'

'Of course,' a voice say, from out of nowhere. 'You've gained the physical attributes of a draconic form, not its mind. That still remains your own — for now.'

You could have sworn there wasn't anyone there a moment ago. The scent's there too, now. Turning swiftly, what you'd hoped would be an elegant whirl turns into a slightly awkward shuffle as your mind still insists that you only have two feet.

The tail comes close to knocking your visitor over. It seems to have a mind of its own. But the newcomer doesn't flinch as your tail passes over his head with mere inches to spare. Nor does he so much as bat an eye when, a few moments later, he comes face to face with your snout.

Your vision going out of focus, you have to back up a few steps before you can see him clearly. A very tall man, you think — though from your height everyone now looks short — and dressed in what looks like robes flowing in the breeze. Oddly enough, his sleek, long, black hair barely moves despite the wind. He regards you solemnly.

'It would appear that you were caught in an unexpected feedback loop from old Rundelswollp's transmigratory experiment,' he says.

He walks around you as your narrowed eyes never leave him, oblivious to any danger you might represent. Or, perhaps, confident enough in his own ability that having several tons of dragon on his doorstep (though you can't see any doors in the vicinity) isn't worth much more than a raised eyebrow in the grand scheme of things.

For the time being, it's probably best to believe it's the second, but that doesn't mean you're willing to trust him.

'A most unfortunate circumstance, indeed,' he says as he keeps pacing. 'My most sincere apologies. It would appear that the transference is somewhat, ahem, unstable in nature.'

'What?'

You rumble threateningly. If he thinks he can intimidate you with all this wizard-speak, he's got the wrong dragon. But he *does* appear to understand you and between that, the robes he's wearing, and the way he speaks, you're guessing he's some sort of arcane user. A spellslinger. You try to keep him in your sights. You never quite know where they stand, wizards.

'Go ahead, I'm listening,' you grumble. Whatever else he is, he's either very used to dragons and might give you a few tips, or they are more common in this world than you'd have expected. Turn to **112**

Not willing to trust the word of a stranger or a wizard and definitely not a strange wizard, you throw open your wings and claw your way into the sky. Turn to **226**

So, this is all their doing, is it? You let out a mighty roar and lunge forwards, jaws agape, frills quivering. Turn to **403**

206

A broken trebuchet goes up in flames as you pass over. Then another. Why anyone would bring siege equipment to a battle like this you can't imagine, but-they-make-for-easy-targets.

Letting out a mighty roar you scour the left flank with fire. Horses try to bolt. Men fall over, wild-eyed. For a moment the field turns into even more chaos than before. Amongst that, you land, trying to avoid squashing anyone by accident. If only you can make them all see sense.

Then with mighty yells, both sides swarm over you. They might not be well-armed, but they're tenacious and they just won't stop.

Congratulations, you achieved what you wanted. You've united the armies

— against you!

207

It must be disoriented because it's heading straight for Aawk Rock, not the depths of the marine trench. It's moving fast. So fast both you and the gryphons struggle to keep up. What reserves of power this beast must have, you think.

It doesn't do it any good, though, for its next opponent becomes Aawk Rock itself. Standing firm and unyielding, the monster fish rams it at full speed.

The air around you fills with all the happy sounds you've ever heard birds make and many that you haven't. Through the calls and warbles cut several, almost roar-like, eruptions that rolls over the island. You'll all eat well tonight.

Almost as an afterthought, this all probably means you bested the third challenge. Turn to **183**

Gryphon companion: *Several of the gryphons veer close to you. One of them detaches from the flight, coming to dance circles around you. Turn to* **250**

208

After hours of flying over nothing but fields of ripening (now burning) wheat, rye, and other cereals and assorted greens — along with the occasional hovel or hamlet (now smoking) with people (now screaming) and livestock (now running) — you finally come upon the city you've been searching for. The great city of Zuri.

It stands in the daylight, sparkling against the horizon, on a hill. No wait, it *is* the hill. Row upon row of white houses, ivory towers straining against the sky, and bright sandstone pillars and ornaments almost as large as you.

There are wimples streaming in the wind above golden domes. The whole city is floating on a shimmer of hot air until you fly in closer.

It's not even noon yet, but the unforgiving suns are already growing stronger. The smell of scorched earth and warm stone mix and rise.

You circle on the updraft created by the city, watching it from above. It looks rich. You decide it's yours now.

To survey your new domain, you choose to land on the tallest structure you can find. It's only fitting that that puts you right in the centre of the circular city. Right where you should be. Turn to **398**

You decide to land by the gates to the city. After all, that's what they're there for, right? Turn to **249**

209

While these foothills show all signs of being utterly devoid of life (usually a sure sign *something* is living there), some of the lesser mountains sport the occasional tilled field. But there is no sign of the city the Archmage spoke about. Did he send you on a wild goose chase? A game of "who can fool the dragon best?" You let out a deep rumble at the thought of being made a fool of. But he's been right so far, so you decide to take a closer look.

Your nostrils pick up the smell of charred wood and coal. Smoke. You can't see it, yet, but your nostrils aren't lying. You decide to follow it. Turn to **243**

More inclined to trust your eyes than anything else, you can see small sheds dotted about in the landscape. You would have missed them, for they have grass and wildflowers growing on their roofs, had it not been for your excellent eyesight. Turn to **355**

210

You'd hoped to catch them by surprise, but instead it's you who are caught off guard.

No. Best to retreat for now. You can always come back later — after you've gotten your paws on some extra armour or spells. Turn to **388**

Perhaps you can turn the tide of battle in your favour? Turn to **140**

211

The valley you find isn't far from your last location but it doesn't look like anyone has made it into a home. You can't understand why, because, to your eyes, it shimmers marvellously in soft greens and flowers of every colour.

The buzzing of bees going about their business would have annoyed you when human, but now you barely even notice it, except as a droning sound at the back of your ears, and one persistent bee that flies into your left nostril needing to be snorted out again.

You can't wait to go explore the valley. Turn to **161**

Cat companion: *Chaos, who's been riding on your shoulders, leaps down amongst the flowers. Turn to* **258**

212

The traveller is absolutely covered in grey and brown and black dust. From the floppy hat drooping over his face to the duster coat mashup, to hide here they'd only need to lie down or stand still and they'd be missed by any but the most eagle-eyed scout. But they didn't fool your nose. Sweeping off his hat, the traveller flaps it against his thigh a couple of times and, as you bend forwards, smacks you with it right between your nostrils, again.

'Personal Space, dragon!'

Grumbling an irritated 'sorry,' you're surprised, again, when the man gives you a small nod and tucks his long, brown hair, or fur, back in under his hat.

'Didn't expect company, not out here,' he says. Don't suppose you're heading back into town?'

You manage to negotiate a ride into the nearest settlement in return for some-thing to eat. Turn to **181**

Ignore the traveller and return without the reagent. Turn to **151**

You're so incensed by being treated like an overgrown lizard that you whip around, swiping the man from his feet with your tail. He makes a very satisfactory 'thunk' sound as he's crushed by the weight. Turn to **202**

213

You raise your head, taking in the new world around you. What could there possibly be out there that you'd need to worry about? Nothing. Nothing at all. Flexing your wing muscles, you pump your wings, blowing away rocks and dirt.

It takes a few tries and a few very bumpy landings, but eventually you claw your way into the sky.

It's a new world out there, and you have no qualms about exploring it all alone. Turn to **116**

214

YIKES!

As you scrape away the moss with your talons, up comes a large skull. As you watch, the dark moisture on it fades in the warm air until it's dry and bleached and looks more like the skulls you're used to seeing.

It's not quite as big as yours, but it IS a dragon's skull. Something around here can kill dragons. *Has* killed dragons.

Suddenly the shadows of the forest don't feel as cool as they do suspicious. Underneath your armour, your insides are tying themselves into three types of knots.

No wonder the dwarves didn't want to come here. No way you're sticking around somewhere where dragons can get killed. No thanks. Your great eyes roll back into your skull. Turn to **201**

215

It's not hard to walk around the forest. The treeline ends rather abruptly, so all you have to do is to stay to one side and plod on like another cart horse — an analogy you don't care much for when it pops into your mind.

Hoping to come across a younger specimen, one you can actually uproot and fly all the way back to the mountain without dropping it, you keep searching. Eyeing the stout trees on your left you wonder if you can. You might have four sets with which to hold on to it, but they're mighty big trees and if they're anything like ironwoods, they'll be even heavier than they look.

As you keep on searching, you eventually happen upon — not the tree you're looking for — but a knight. A very forlorn looking knight at that, clanging armour and all. He even has a lance, though this is wedged firmly in the ground at an odd angle. What could he possibly have been aiming for? Unchivalrous earthworms?

The knight might be armoured to boot — it must be boiling in there — but he's very sans horse and, curling your upper lip at the sight, he doesn't look like much of a threat. Maybe he'll be able to direct you to the right tree? Turn to **324**

Leaving the knight well alone — tales of old and all that — you keep looking for the reagent yourself. Turn to **314**

216

Turns out that stalking prey in concealment through the underbrush isn't really something a dragon is suited for. You keep snagging on trees. If you want to catch anything you're going to have to do it from the air.

But wait, something sparkles up ahead.

You find the glitter between the swaying tree crowns irresistible. Drawn to it like a moth to a flame, you decide to investigate. Turn to **152**

Despite every bone in your body wanting to investigate the mysterious sparkles, another rumble from your stomach decides for you. With a low growl at the unfairness of it all, you turn towards where you smelled the deer. Turn to **107**

217

You find a nice, serene valley a few removed from any battle. It's filled with a gentle greenness and more flowers than you have ever seen in one place. Clearly, no one ever comes here.

It looks ideal for a dragon's snooze — no knights or other bothersome individuals to, well, bother you. You turn in a circle a couple of times then, flicking the end of your tail over your long muzzle, you breathe a sigh of relief.

*Your dreams turn from pleasant serendipity when getting invaded by alarm-clocks. Several of them. All their hands are flashing by, moving like evil mouths chasing you, hopping and bouncing, trying to eat you. Turn to **347***

*Your dreams are soon filled with the most wondrous creatures imaginable. Everything from fabled phoenixes to tiny, talking mice, all set to harpsichord music played by faeries flickering in and out of existence. Turn to **138***

218

The heat rises around you, but you barely feel it. It takes a lot to make stone burn and you adjust the strength of your flames. No sense in burning the city to the ground — who's going to pay you tribute then?

Swivelling your head slowly, the fire licks the world with orange and red and white tongues. Windows go up in smoke. Armour clatters to the ground, nothing more than molten slags. The screaming intensifies. This pleases you.

*Swords and arrows proving woefully inadequate against a dragon of your stature, you decide to ignore them after a few more outbursts of rage calculated to send terror running rampant through the streets. A place this size must have an equally well-endowed treasure chamber. Right? Turn to **117***

219

It's a good thing the spells wear off after a while, but you're going to think twice about entering forbidding-looking towers from now on. You might be magic, as all dragons are, but spells and potions are a different matter.

*Maybe it's best to try and see if those dwarves are around here somewhere, anyway? Turn to **355***

*After several circuits around the mountainous region you still find no trace of your quarry. Only one thing left to do then... Turn to **193***

220

Kobolds might be immune to dragonfire, but they're certainly not immune to spikes coming at them at speed. The lash of your tail knocks it over, impaling it. You pound the tip of your tail against the ground to rid it of the bleeding carcass.

*Snarling, you whip around, swiping two other attackers you hadn't known were there a moment ago, down out of the branches. Turn to **251***

*Did you enjoy the sound of horn crunching through thick skin? Turn to **239***

221

For a moment, you think you see something. Then you blink and it's gone.

*There does seem to be all kinds of small critters about, but you're so big they don't see you as a threat and ignore you. Guess you're not the first dragon to come through these parts. Turn to **362***

222

Going tree hunting, it takes several days, as the dragon flies, before you even spot the signs you've been told to look out for. It's like the entire continent is covered in foliage. You've never seen so many trees crammed into one space before and they stand so tightly that you can't even find anywhere to land until the green canopy below begins to resemble the ironwoods growing by the dwarves' mountain.

The descent shows branch after branch disappearing upwards into the canopy. Guess the dwarves forgot to mention that these trees are even bigger than you are. "Friggin' enormous" doesn't even come close.

Thankfully, these woods are skirted by narrow patches of grasslands, so you manage to land without breaking anything, including your precious wings, but if you want to be able to carry anything back, you're going to have to find a younger tree.

You spotted some lighter green and orange deeper in the woods as you passed over earlier. Thinking that's your best bet, you try to enter the forest. Turn to **178**

The border between woods and hills should have plenty of new growth, you hope and decide to take your chance on that. Turn to **215**

223

When you gaze down into the still waters, at first you see nothing but blue sky and the occasional palm tree. Then you spot a swirling globe of fire. You blink. It vanishes. Then it's back. It's an eye. Your eye. You realize that what's blocking everything else out is you.

You're one impressive dragon now. Your horns are even curvier than when you first laid eyes upon your body; your talons are stronger, more dangerous; your frills brighter; your frown deeper; your dragon form more, well, dragony.

But, no matter how impressed you might be, there's no one around here and you crave their recognition. Their fear. The desire burns in you. So you leave the oasis and take wing once again. Turn to **125**

*You soon grow bored. Deciding to keep exploring — still hoping to stumble across one of those great tombs of old — you take wing. Dark eyes of every colour watch you leave. Turn to **368***

224

As you draw closer to the cave, the opening looks less scruffy and a whole lot smaller. You'd be hard pressed to fit your whole head in there. It's as you peer at it, trying to decide what to do next, that you notice the sign to the left of the entrance.

"Visitors, ring bell."

How peculiar, you think. After several attempts, the bell pull being rather too small for you, you tap it with one of your talons. The bell rings out.

Once. Twice. Three times, the bell tolls.

Still, there is no reply from within.

*Nothing to do but wait then, you sigh. Turn to **241***

*Bored by all the waiting, you fall asleep. Turn to **155***

225

Once you deem you're far enough away, you slow down and begin to check every bone and spine, plating, scale, and horn for damage. Something feels quite uncomfortable, not to mention hot, and, rubbing against some stout rock dislodges a scale lodged between your own, aglow from within, the size of your right paw. It's not a heart-of-fire, but it's close enough you think.

*Hoping the scale will be somewhat useful, you don't fancy returning and battling it out with the coulee, you return to the dwarves. Turn to **304***

*You toss the scale. It's not what you're looking for. Turn to **151***

226

The winds are favourable and you're soon lost amongst the clouds. The only thing you need to worry about is what fun to have first. Looking down, there is a vast world below — the only thing you're missing is a map.

You're going to be the greatest adventurer this world has ever known, you just know it. What could possibly stand in the way of a dragon? Turn to **116**

Who was that mysterious person you saw anyway? Does it matter? You have a whole world to explore. Still, deep in your heart's chambers there's a tiny, nagging, doubt. Maybe you'll run into them again sometime and you can ask them then? Turn to **200**

227

The trees eventually part to reveal … a stone wall. It's quite high and you need to stand on your haunches, stretching your neck to the utmost, to peek over it. Oh great. More trees!

But wait, these aren't just green leaves, they're filled with fruits. Glistening red and yellow apples, rich purple plums, and orange peaches and more fill the garden beyond the stone wall with tantalizing scents. The berry bushes are heavy and ripe. Rhubarb adds a tangent.

But that isn't anything compared to the one you don't recognize. You feel your mouth watering and steal over the wall like a scaly thief in the night.

You pick a fruit here and there and pop them in your mouth but that smell leads you on, deeper into the garden, until you stand before a group of trees growing taller and brighter than all those around them. Their leaves glitter with a bronze tint that remind you of autumn and their branches are heavy with large fruit that could have been a cross between an apple and a watermelon if they didn't look like they were solid gold.

Snatching a golden fruit from the nearest tree, one soon turns into many. You just can't stop eating them. Turn to **141**

*Maybe you'll try just one before you leave. There's no harm in that, right? Turn to **394***

228

The wyvern — a green-flecked creature with a frilly neck — is significantly smaller than you are. You should have smelled it before you even entered these caverns — if you'd known what wyverns smelled like that is.

The stand-off feels like it goes on forever, though it's probably not even a minute. As you close in on the creature, it launches itself at you.

In such an enclosed space its smaller size gives it an advantage and during the battle you break stalagmites and stalactites to the right and left as you swing your head wildly trying to capture it in your maws. Its claws dig into you again and again as it continues to screech. You've invaded its home. It's not going to go down without a fight.

Then, a lucky strike. Your paw catches its wing in flight, dragging it to the ground and crushing the annoying pest underneath your paw's much bigger weight.

*Now that your eyes have acclimatized, you see that there are several more tunnels leading off the main cavern. There might be thieves hiding there, you think. Best to exterminate them early on. Turn to **262***

*You stash what remains of your treasure the best you can, far from the foul-smelling nest you spot tucked against the far wall and decide you better find out where that trail nearby leads after all — there could be treasure thieves about. Turn to **129***

229

It's quite the journey home and you land, rather unceremoniously, and quite hard, on a wooden porch. The only thing is, it's not *your* wooden porch.

Rolling off it, you rub your eyes, wondering where you ended up this time. You hope it's not too far from home. Blinking in the flickering light from a car that passes by, you brush yourself off and take a good look at where you are.

It's dark, so it takes a while before you begin to spot them. The shapes of things. They're not as they should be. The Archmage might have managed to send you back to the right world. Looks like he didn't quite manage to send you back to the right time…

230

It all sounds pretty out of your league, really. And, quite frankly, you're not keen on being used as a fuse.

*It takes a great deal more talking and a far more generous offer on their part before you're willing to consider what they're asking of you. Turn to **402***

*Nope, this isn't for you. They can take their trouble and stuff them. You spread your wings and, bored, leap into the sky, leaving the dwarves tumbling in your wake. Turn to **193***

231

But no matter how you pull, you can't shift the crystal. Not even a smidgen.

*Stupid thing must be enchanted, you snort. The sage must have known that. He's probably laughing his socks off right now — if he'd had any socks that was. Turn to **156***

232

If you want that tree, it looks like you're going to have to fight the wyrm for it. Maybe you can lure it away while Sir Chopalot retrieves the sword?

Locking eyes with the wyrm, you lunge to the left. To the right. Distracting it, that's the key. All you need is one good bite on that scaly neck, and the wyrm is pretty much all *neck. Turn to* **336**

Snapping your jaws shut, you circle the tree like a very armoured, annoyed, cat, ready to pounce. Turn to **396**

233

As the group levels out, many straining for breath, Lightwing blinks her large, soulful eyes as if this is merely all just another vaguely interesting thing to happen today. You're wondering if they're using a spell or something — there's no way their leisurely approach can be natural. Even the leaders look like the climb took a lot out of them.

Then, one by one, the gryphons roll and begin to dive, wings tucked tightly, tightly against their bodies. Faster and faster they go. Turn to **166**

234

Passing by several more of the glowing niches you finally come upon a cavern so large even you are lost for words. Immense doesn't even cover it. It seems to have been some sort of hall once upon a time. The walls are all smooth, with semi-circular pillars at regular intervals and heavy carvings decorating a cartouche running around the circumference.

In the middle of the grand hall, there stands three stone sarcophagi.

There has to be more to this than mere decoration. No one goes to all this much trouble without having something to hide. You eye the sarcophagi. They don't look so tough. Turn to **176**

With a huff, you return to the main cave. Who cares about a lot of boring old stone anyway? Turn to **158**

235

Slowing down, you flap hard to stay in place once you're over the fishing vessel. At the sight of you, the deck turns into frantic, disorganized chaos as everyone is running and pulling at everything. Shouts, yells, even curses, drift up. They're soon followed by broken bits of a wooden taffrail and a bucket that hits you on the muzzle.

That was unfriendly, you think, ears burning. They could just have told you, 'no thanks.' Turn to **360**

236

From the air, you eventually spy a tall tower poking above the forest. It's not anywhere near the mountain where you're expected, but it looks interesting. You veer away from your course and, as you get closer to the tower, it proves to be built of large, roughly hewn, blocks of grey stone. It's also more than large enough for you to be able to land on the ledge so conveniently jutting out just below the pointed roof.

This looks familiar, you think, as you peek in through the opening. There are shelves of jars and bottles. Books are strewn over every surface, including the floor, so you have to pick your way carefully as you tiptoe through what is clearly an arcane study. Some flutter open as you pass them, a faint glow emanating from their pages.

But your eyes are drawn to the shelf above the ornate, varnished oak throne, or, more accurately, to the four containers thereupon. A tingling sensation when you lock your gaze on them suggests that these four probably have more magic in them than everything in the rest of the room combined.

You can't see what it contains, but that's what draws you to the stone-decanter. Turn to **144**

The crystal bottle with an emerald-coloured stopper and faintly glowing green liquid looks the most interesting. Turn to **267**

Sitting like a dark, fat, toad, the round glass bottle is almost empty. Turn to **297**

A fourth bottle, smaller than the others, sits under a hefty layer of dust. Obviously not an everyday item, you think. Turn to **187**

237

Your head snaps around at the scream. What is that fool of a thing trying to make you do? Oh, right. It's a *wizard's* familiar, right? Of course, it's going to take *their* side. You knew you couldn't trust some rotten, little piece of fluff like that.

Cat companion: *You snarl at the pesky, little critter. Chaos, small as he is, clings on to your shoulder spikes and hisses back. Turn to* **334**

Gryphon companion: *You lunge at the feathered flyer. Turn to* **281**

238

Draconic laughter fills the garden. Between the fits of twisting stomachs, you're laughing too hard. Tears stream from your eyes. You feel silly for having been afraid of something so small.

'Funny you think this is? Who dares disturb my garden? Who dares? A lizard with wings!'

Now, that is more than a little insulting, but you're too busy laughing to swat at the creature when the small man raps his stick in the ground and booms, 'BEGONE!' 'Begone, foul creature. Begone, thief!'

The earth shakes when the stick hits it. The voice rolling like thunder, reverberates around your eardrums until they're ready to burst.

Without asking you, your legs begin to scrabble madly to get the rest of you out of there before the ground opens up and swallows you. Turn to **303**

239

You snap at anyone foolish enough to be in the vicinity. This ends now!

Your eyes begin to turn a swirling, angry red. Turn to **372**

240

Breaking a few trees for kindling, there's soon a roaring bonfire going. Curling up around it, the heat splashes pleasantly over your body, the tip of your tail twitching in tune to the dancing flames.

Dinner had come curtsey of the satchel the Archmage gifted you and you're wondering if there might be something else interesting in there. Normally, bags like that don't yield chicken drumsticks the size of an ostrich. It doesn't taste much like ostrich. On the other hand, it doesn't taste much like chicken, either.

You stick in a claw, then a paw and keep going until you've buried your arm all the way up to the elbow in the small leather satchel. No wonder all those things fit — it really *was* bigger on the inside.

You wake up the next morning. Yawning so widely that a small armoured chariot would have been able to drive in and park, you smack your lips together. You're hungry … again.

That Archmage said dragons don't need to eat often, but you realize you haven't had a bite since you were turned into one, asides from the drumsticks. What about breakfast? Turn to **341**

Grumbling, and no one can grumble in the morning quite like a dragon, you blink away sleep with bleary eyes. Realizing that you're on the clock, you decide to dive right into everything. Turn to **200**

241

For several hours, nothing happens. Maybe the inhabitants are out?

Promises or not, you get bored and leave. Turn to **146**

242

The place keeps getting smaller and narrower as you go along.

When it starts scraping against the scales on your shoulders, you relent.

There's nothing to do but to back up, carefully. Turn to **382**

243

Looking (well, sniffing, actually) around for the source of the smoke, it turns out to be emitted by a thicket of bushes, brambles, and thorns. The bushes don't look as if they're on fire, so you figure that the source of the smoke is somewhere below. But sweeping everything away with a swipe of your powerful paw comes to an abrupt stop that shakes you in your very bones. The biological chimney is protected by some very stout ironwood trees.

As you eye the entire arrangement, trying to make up your mind if you should set fire to it or not, there's a loud, 'ahem!' from behind you.

You nearly jump out of your scales.

Whirling around, you're faced with a tiny individual dressed in little but a loincloth and a leather headband so large that the only reason it doesn't fall off is because it's snagged on the creature's huge, pointy ears.

It looks too small to be a threat, but the ridiculous creature scared you and you flame before you even realize what you're doing. Turn to **351**

A dragon should be able to be diplomatic as well as a towering inferno. Maybe this little thing will know where the city is? Turn to **266**

Do you have tail spikes? If so, now might be a good time to use them. Turn to **220**

244

While fuming, you're losing height. Your tail drags in the water. You don't even notice before something big and heavy clamps its jaws around it and dives, yanking you right out of the sky and into the sea.

Giant monsterfish: 1

Dragon: 0

What a way for an adventure to end. Fish food.

245

Three of the biggest gryphons take the lead, climbing steadily. Some of the younger ones are striving to keep up, with you taking the position at the rear. For now, they fly almost in silence. The only sounds are of muscles and wind and feathers and the sea churning far below.

*You've long since left the highest point on the island behind you. In fact, it's getting harder and harder to breathe. Spots are beginning to shimmer before your eyes. Turn to **381***

Gryphon Companion: *Risking a glance to the left — you don't want to crash into anyone up here — the wind ruffles through Lightwing's feathers. You can't help but notice it's not nearly as strong as that which the others are struggling against, even at this height. How peculiar. Turn to **233***

246

Still feeling quite full, you wonder what the world has in store for you. After a good night's sleep, wasn't it about time things got exciting around here? Your grin displays an array of sharp fangs that'd send an army scampering for the hills if they didn't know you. It's mischievous but oh-so-filled with anticipation.

There's a promising tint to the horizon. A sun — no, several suns — *some barely more than mere hints of a different colour against the sky —* are rising, turning the world into soft pastel colours you didn't think existed outside of movies.

*Flaring your wings, you flex them, picking up a beat and launching into the sky. You have challenges to complete. Turn to **110***

*Heading out, you pick a direction at random. Turn to **362***

Eyeing the iron doors you're led up to somewhat apprehensively, they look far too tight a squeeze for you, your eyes widen as, with a grinding noise, seams appear in the mountain and what had moments before looked like mere walls of rock and rubble, swing outwards.

Never mind fitting you, you'd have been able to march *three* dragons through there side by side. Craning your neck to take everything in as the dwarves lead you further into the mountain, you can't believe how big everything is. The same goes for the forge, though you only know it is one because the dwarves says so: it looks like the illicit offspring between a giant's plumbing system and a stonemason's descent into madness.

An important-looking dwarf with a grey beard reverentially takes the reagent and places it at the focal point after which everyone turns and looks at you expectantly. You realize that you do need to light it too and doing so saps every ounce of strength from you, but, as you wobble back outside, the furnace burns with unyielding flame once more.

With much bowing, you're treated to several items of treasure, including an armband in gold. It's carved with intricate details too small for you to see, but it slides comfortably over your left arm and you admire how it glitters in the sun.

But you glow with pride as you take from the dwarves that which you were promised. It's some sort of strange, purple rock with crystal veins. You turn it over and over and wonder what's so special about it, but the main thing is, you realize with elation, is that you've successfully completed your second challenge.

You do wish you knew what purpose these challenges serve. So far they don't seem to have anything in common. There's got to be something else out there ... More ... Turn to **211**

Just one more challenge left. You can't wait. Turn to **193**

Looking down at what your new friends just handed you, a very large draconic frown appears as your heavy brows knot in consternation. This makes no sense. You want answers, and you want them now. Turn to **172**

248

Before you know it, your companion has swooped down and plucked the wet bundle from the maws of the ocean, their wingtips sending up ocean spray as they struggle to gain altitude again. Lightwing warbles at you, banking gently towards the island where you're met by a multitude of gryphons and two very grateful parents who immediately begin to warm and clean the bedraggled piece of fluff.

*You didn't expect there to be quite this many. Surely such a small, barren looking place can support them all? Turn to **270***

249

There seems to be a few parties on the road leading up to the city's main gate.

*They look tiny and vulnerable from up here. You send a fireball in their direction, just to get them out of the way. Then you wing your way over to the gate itself and land in a blast of air. Turn to **349***

*You hover over the gate, pondering where it would be best to land, when your keen senses catches sight and scent of something that you can't quite place. It doesn't smell bad, but it sends shivers down your spine. Changing your mind, you decide to aim for a smaller settlement instead. Turn to **380***

250

Lightwing grins at you when she flies by. At least you'd swear she's grinning — it's hard to tell with that beak. Gryphons might be able read each other's expressions but they've had plenty of practice. They do show you how to carve sizeable chunks from the, now very dead, monster fish, and the air fill with the squabble of birds and gryphons as news of the food spread.

The birds are far more numerous than the gryphons and far more annoying.

*You snap after several of them as they try to use your head as a landing platform. Turn to **183***

251

Something else rustles in the bushes. Then, out of the greenery, from behind the rocks, from within the crevices, they come. Kobolds. An army of kobolds.

*They have you outnumbered, but you're a dragon. You can take them. Turn to **135***

Gryphon companion:** You glance over at Lightwing, who screeches and leaps forward. You hope she can find another way out of this situation than tearing each other to shreds. Turn to **405

252

The water feels so good. The pool's level rose and flooded a lot when you plunged right into it, but it's cool and comforting and refreshing to drink. You gulp down several gallons before you start taking an interest in where you've ended up.

There are no random remains of rope. No pieces of cloth stolen by enterprising marsupials. There's not even a carved cartouche in sight.

Well, you're not going to build your reputation out here. You can see that. To be intimidating and impressive, there has to be someone to intimidate and impress. When you think desert, your mind turns to mighty structures rising from the sand, to burial chambers filled with gifts (to you), and processions in the dark.

Sand isn't what you wanted to impress.

After a few hours rest, you stretch your legs, shake the tension from your tail, and return to your element — the sky. Turn to **125**

Eventually you abandon your bath and curl up, intending to sleep until the worst of the blinding light out here has given up and gone home. But as the surface of the water grows still, it draws you to it. Turn to **223**

253

There's a great milling about, but, oddly enough, you don't notice a single gryphon in the sky. They must be waiting for something. But what? And what has it got to do with you?

You try to flex a wing and accidentally knock into one of the many gryphons. This one, a handsome male, several shades darker in his leonine coat than many others here, gives you a steely eyed glare — a feat for which gryphons are well-equipped. Your companion clicks her beak and the male reluctantly moves away, tail swishing.

Then, one by one, the gryphons begin taking off. But they don't leave. Instead, they circle again and again until only you and Lightwing remain earthbound.

Lightwing nips you, in a friendly sort of way, telling you to get a move on. You still have no idea what you're doing here but feel it's best not to argue. Turn to **199**

Brow furrowing, you watch them for several minutes wondering what this all has to do with what you're supposed to fetch from Aawk Rock. Turn to **273**

254

OUCH!

A beast has chopped off several feet of your tail. Anger fills your veins. This thing dares to hurt you, does it? You're the one who's supposed to be the hero of the story.

Whipping around, your jaws snap shut on nothing. Whatever this beast is, whomever they might be, they're well-versed in combat and despite their hulking stature, they're much smaller than you, but they give you such a sound beating that you'll be feeling it in your bones for weeks.

In the process, you've crushed what little remained of the vegetable plots.

You slink away in defeat. Turn to **146**

255

Your eyes are fierce, almost burning from within. You roll one experimentally, but no, you can't see your face unless you look into the pond sideways, both eyes set towards the side of your head. They also sit underneath a pair of heavy brow ridges that's going to make scowling at your enemies very easy. As long as they're not standing straight in front of you that is.

Your body is powerfully built yet lean, and there are spikes *everywhere*. Small spikes. Huge spikes. Curved. Rolled. Extra pointy. Someone clearly ordered the lot, you think, as you admire your reflection.

And let's not even get started on your fangs, which you bare. Two rows, in both the upper and lower jaw. Nope. Smiling doesn't make you the least bit more friendly looking — it even sends a few nearby creatures that have begun to return after you appeared scurrying away again.

Turning your snout into the wind, even the movement of your nostrils, layered with flaps and underlying flesh, would send most armies running, as you sniff a couple of times. There's something interesting ... over there. Turn to **213**

Now, there's the small issue of where you are. Not that it bothers you, but maybe there is someone around to ask? You can always eat them afterwards if they make a fuss. Turn to **205**

256

Looks like the remains of two once vast armies are still slugging it out. Much of what wooden equipment either side brought with them lies broken along with scores of their dead, amongst whose bodies the battle continues.

From your height, what shouts there are jumble together with the clangs of swords and shields and spears — the only weapons still in play.

Both sides are so dirty, so covered in blood and mud that you can't even tell them apart — or if everyone is still fighting merely because everyone else is still fighting, when anyone that was once an enemy has died or fled long ago.

*Buzz the battlefield. Turn to **263***

*This will take a more personal approach to put an end to, you think. Turn to **206***

257

Turns out there aren't many other dragons out here amongst the sand. In fact, it's years before you even lay eyes on another one and they take one look at you and beat their wings so hard you thought they might fall off, to get away from you. You hadn't laughed so hard in ages.

You hound the caravan trades. Make the occasional dash into the mountains when you feel like more action. Your spines and horns keep on growing. Indeed, every year another seems to bud.

In time, you'll bear greater resemblance to someone's intoxicated nightmares than a dragon, but no one seeks you out, out here. No heroes. No mercenaries. And, as you still can't really cast magic all that well, thankfully no wizards or sorcerers either. You rule all of the Sandsea with an iron paw.

258

You watch the cat chase a butterfly fluttering past. As he runs into the field of pink and white flowers, he stops and bats a paw at the one the butterfly lands on.

Chaos sneezes and runs back to you. Scrambling back onto your shoulders, your companion hiss.

Snorting with draconic laughter at the grey cat being bested by a tiny butterfly, you start exploring. Turn to **126**

Grumbling something about never being allowed to do what you want, you heed Chaos' insistence that you both leave, now, and return to the sky. Turn to **193**

259

Curling up, the cat is shaking like a leaf the whole time. When you spot a lonesome farmstead with some nice looking barns you set down, careful to not be spotted. Not a hard feat as it's now grown quite dark.

Gently, you unlatch the barn doors to let the cat in. At first, it doesn't want to go — then, as if realizing the alternative, it disappears into the semi-darkness.

You saw some mountains earlier and you think you can still remember what direction they were in. Turn to **358**

Onwards and upwards it is. Turn to **153**

260

The rumble begins deep in your chest. It spreads to your arms and legs and tail until your whole being is quivering. You feel like a very large, very angry cat, only larger and a great deal angrier.

There's a heat rising around your heart and smoke beginning to rise from your nostrils.

Cat companion: *Chaos clings on, his face a mix of horror and disappointment, as you stomp off looking for something to get your teeth into. Turn to* **357**

Now, what's around here that's good enough for a dragon to eat? Turn to **269**

261

You call out to your companion again. Surely, they must have battled creatures like this before?

The gryphon warbles back, but she continues circling high above. The heat rising from the caldera is increasing and Lightwing is struggling not to get blown away by the hot air rising as a result. If the gryphon descends to where you are, they'll be cooked. She won't be able to help you with this.

Looks like you're on your own. Bugger. Turn to **370**

262

The places where the wyvern bit you throb. The pesky critter must have been poisonous. But even without that, you still ache from where all the boulders fell on you earlier. So, you carefully stash what treasure you still possess in the wyvern's nest — only to discover that it too, apparently, had an eye for the shinies. Excellent. More for you.

You eye the other tunnels warily. You should probably explore them all to be on the safe side, but which one should you start with?

Tunnel three looks unassuming — and a tight fit too. Turn to **338**

Tunnel two seems to have been used before. It even has a dint to its floor from years and years of something walking back and forth. Turn to **322**

There's a strange smell wafting in from tunnel one. One you wouldn't normally associate with tunnels. Turn to **286**

263

Your wings sing as you buzz the battlefield.

But those fighting below you are so intent on their enemy, who they think are their enemy, that they don't even notice you. It's a good thing for them that you're not evil. You could have blasted them into oblivion and they'd have been none the wiser.

Tired and a little depressed at the state of things, you leave the battlefield, instead looking for a place to nap and dream more pleasant dreams. Turn to **217**

Apparently, a more forceful approach is needed, you think, gritting your teeth. Well, you are a dragon ... There should be "something" you can do that they can't, surely. Turn to **206**

264

You gather up what you've gotten so far and, with a blast from your wings that knocks over several buildings, you take off. Circling once over the city, to remind them who is boss, you roar a couple of times, shift your weight, and set your eyes on the horizon.

You'll be back, but for now you'll need to find somewhere safe to squirrel away all your new shinies.

So, what do you see? Where will you head next? There must be something suitable out there. You scan the world beneath you with cold eyes. Turn to **380**

265

You flare your wings and stretch your neck so far it feels almost like you can touch the sky. You roar again. It's so liberating, getting every pent of frustration and tension in your body and expelling it by force.

You're almost ready to fly away when there's a loud, 'ahem,' from behind you. 'There are, of course, some conditions to this offer.'

Oh bugger, you might have known the serious-looking Archmage wasn't going to just let you dash off into new adventures without him having a say in the matter. Settling down, you fidget restlessly as Kaheiron begins explaining what your new life will entail.

You grin widely. The tip of your tail twitches. There is so much more to explore. A whole new world. Out There!

266

Huge orbs of rolling colour blink as you arch your proud neck to place your head closer to the small, blue creature. You barely understand a single thing it's saying, but you get the main point. It wants you to wait here. Apparently someone is coming to meet with you.

You wonder who else might live in a mountain like this. The kobold doesn't look the city-building type. Turn to **147**

There's no way something like this would be able to provide any useful information. You decide to move on to the third challenge. Turn to **193**

267

Reaching out for the crystal decanter, as soon as you touch it you're filled with an overwhelming desire to drink it. The compulsion is too strong to fight and you pull desperately at the emerald stopper, then down the contents in a single swallow.

Bam!

Wonderful, you're now a big, fluffy, white bunny the size of four horses, complete with a wobbly pink nose and cottontail. You wrinkle your nose.

Stamping a hind foot, you leap effortlessly through the opening through which you came. Turn to **219**

Good thing you still have paws, you think, as you carefully pull out the stopper from the glass bottle next. Turn to **297**

268

Steadily catching up with the agile, but now heavy, fliers, you find the others have begun circling a wide patch of sea. Round and round they go. Occasionally one will drop a smaller rock. Some gryphons are carrying more than one, swooping back in for another go. Some almost skim the surface, dragging their tails through the waves like giant lures.

The sea here doesn't look any different to you than the bits two hundred metres away and you almost drop your rock when a huge fish so ugly and sizable in appearance you've never before encountered it outside the realm of nightmares, breaches.

Loud squawks and shrill cries echo forth over the sea as the beast snaps at the nearest flyers, who quickly speed out of the way in erratic movements to avoid getting eaten whole. The rest begin to pelt the nightmare fish with every stone and rock they have. It thrashes about, turning the sea into churning white waters of foam and spray and death.

Thinking it's best to leave the fishing to the experts, you hang back. Turn to **327**

Clutching your rock tightly, you dive. Turn to **352**

269

Well, any peasant should know to feed a hungry dragon when one comes to call, you think. Casting about for something edible, your eyes fall on the bellowing oxen, which you proceed to devour. A little stringy, perhaps … but an excellent appetizer. The cow soon goes the same way, as does the couple of goats you manage to sniff out.

Running your tongue over your chops, you debate if you should set fire to the place — it'd certainly wouldn't be anyone's loss and they *did* insult you — but you'd rather go in search of a nice drink. The village well is far too narrow to stick your snout into.

As a reminder of who they belong to, you do set fire to a few of the houses, then turn to leave. Turn to **377**

270

The point you land on is — aside from a slender, precarious, stone pillar worn so thin by weather and wind out here it looks like it might topple over any moment — the highest point on the island. From here, you can practically see all around the island, it's that small. It rises almost vertically from the ocean.

Where you landed also sports the only tufts of grass in existence out here. Doubting that anyone lives out here you gaze around you, and aside from an errant pup, every gryphon here sports fully grown manes and ruffs. Their hindquarters are strong, gleaming in the sun, and they carry with them an aura of quiet confidence, power, and grace.

Or the closest ones to you are, anyway — towards the edges of this little gathering several seem to be involved in games of leaping and running, like tag played by a bunch of kittens with wings.

Welcome to Aawk Rock.

Gryphon companion: The gryphons here seem quite happy to see Lightwing, whom some greet with head-butts and others with what you take is affectionate nibbling. Turn to **253**

So, if no one actually lives around here, then what is everyone doing here? Despite the antics of some, it looks important to you. Turn to **113**

271

'Behold mortal! For I am—'

The Djinn, for all the impressive way he billows out of his prison, peers at you near-sightedly. 'Wait. You are not— Oh, I see.' The moment of confusion passes and he rubs his hands in glee and begins to chant.

'Wait,' you rumble. 'What about my wishes?'

'Wishes?' The Djinn ceases his chanting to laugh uproariously. 'Would you wish to be big? I'll make you wish you were?'

The Djinn snaps his fingers and suddenly you're barely one foot high. You hiss at the Djinn who takes no notice. Turn to **343**

Trying to snarl, you barely manage to squeak. Launching yourself at the cloud man, he merely flows out of the way. Turn to **278**

272

Circling wide, eyes peeled, there doesn't seem to be anything out of the ordinary. Deciding it must have been a trick of the light, you straighten out and, with one mighty wingbeat, push yourself forwards, then let the wind carry you.

At least it looks like the rocky island you're aiming for is much closer now. Turn to **270**

273

Still at a loss, it becomes obvious that whatever you were sent here for, you're not going to get it. Angry and feeling put upon, you take off in a blast of wind.

You're going to give that stupid spellslinger a piece of your mind when you catch him, sending you on this wild goose chase, you growl. Turn to **172**

274

Every time you try to go a little faster, your companion yowls. Balancing precariously on your shoulders, they shoot glares of evil towards the water sloshing against and over you. Guess they don't like getting their paws wet.

This had better all be worth it, you think. Turn to **285**

275

The other dragons soon catch you up. They circle you making rumbling sounds. Sounds that get increasingly agitated when you don't reply. But how can you, you have no idea what they're saying. For all your scales and wings you *look* like a dragon to them, but you don't *speak* dragon.

You can tell they're unhappy with you and you snap at one of them as they glide past you. They move lazily out of the way then fold their wings and dart away, only to appear a little further back. A growl rises up in your throat and your spikes quiver. How dare they? How dare they!?

The fury begins to take you over. You can feel it ripple beneath your muscles. Your skin. Your scales.

Something cold and spiky shoots past your snout. Ouch. That was an iceblast. These dragons don't just shoot flame and fire. You launch yourself at them, your roar reverberating through the heavens. Turn to **397**

276

Everyone in every fantasy movie you've ever seen and every book you've read always seem to favour hunting deer or rabbits, so you figure that if they can do it, so can you. It'd have to be one big bunny though or you'll be spending the rest of the day hunting down enough of them, so you opt for the deer. Besides, you've got the fangs and the claws for it now, not to mention the speed.

You figure you know what they look like and the scent is strong enough that they can't be hard to find. Though, you do worry things might get a little bit messy once you do. Turn to **216**

277

You keep on swimming downwards until your path is blocked by giant rocks from under which blinks several sets of eyelids. What could it be? You're not sure you want to find out, at this size even a carp would be lethal. Why did you shrink, anyway?

As the dark shapes starts moving towards you, you dash away, swimming desperately for the surface. Your lungs are burning and, unable to hold back, you gasp for air only to receive a lungful of water. Your body thrashes about, desperate for an escape. Too bad you run out of oxygen before you ever find one, your body returning to its original size as it sinks to the bottom of the lake to never been seen again.

278

You lash out with a well-taloned paw. You mean to smite this Djinn from the surface of the world. This time the Djinn doesn't even bother moving. You bare your fangs and bear down on him with a vengeance.

Nothing happens. You just flow right through him. Wait. Your paws aren't even touching the ground anymore. They're floating several feet above it. He turned you into a balloon dragon. You're all squeaky tubes and nasal whine, rolling over and over in the air as you try and toast him

The Djinn laughs coldly at your flailing limbs. Then, with another snap of his fingers, you blink out in a flash. Turn to **290**

Years pass before the Djinn tires of the game. Turn to **257**

279

Silly knights. Intelligent monsters. Feisty princesses. What's next? Flying turtles?

Deciding that the ways of the ground-bound folk are just too strange, you leap into the sky. Turn to **153**

Soon, the treetops are nothing but a green carpet beneath you. You pick up speed. You want a real *challenge and it looks like you'll have to travel a bit to get one. Turn to* **110**

280

You plough through the water, a wake sloshing behind you, in increasingly annoyed and faster circles. But no matter how hard you look, there isn't any mysterious submerged entrance for you to find.

*As you circled the castle in the air, you now circle it in the water. Thankfully, the repulsion doesn't exist down here, but your insides are still complaining. Heading back to shore seems like a good idea. Turn to **393***

*Dripping with water, you heave yourself onto the rocky outcrop upon which the castle stands. Wonderful, now you're just faced with walls that go up and up and up and, from where you stand, don't seem to contain a single window large enough for you to force your body through. Turn to **285***

281

Your jaws snap shut where your companion was just a moment ago. The gryphon rolls out repeatedly as you snap and snarl chasing their tail. An eerie, noisy game of cat-and-mouse ensues high in the sky.

*The gryphon barely manages to escape from your first charge, it's filled with such fury. It becomes talon against talon. Fangs against beak. Then, your former companion misjudges a turn and your heavy body slams into hers. The impact knocks her towards the ground and before she can recover, you drop down on them with every bit of your snarling menace. Her body is squashed to pulp between you and the rocks below. Turn to **298***

*You might be bigger. You might be heavier. But in this battle, those very advantages turn against you. You can't even get within blasting range of the agile gryphon who keeps taunting you with shrill cries. Hovering, you stop the chase. Spitting a final bit of defiance her way, you turn and head out of there — swivelling your head over your shoulders repeatedly to make sure the dastardly creature doesn't follow you. Turn to **392***

282

You lick your chops. That was surprisingly tasty. Maybe taste is like wisdom, you acquire more of it as you age?

There appears a reddish glint in your eyes. Looks like things are finally getting fun around here. Turn to 208

283

As you watch, the brown blob is swallowed by the biggest fish you've ever seen. That could have been you, if you'd been closer. Lucky you.

You point your muzzle towards the island again. Turn to 194

284

You decide to help Sir Chopalot even though you didn't get the tree. He did show you where it was, after all.

Dropping him off at the nearest village (after a fair bit of shouting, the knight apparently not having much of a head for heights, not when it's speeding along beneath him in a blur), the metal man is soon surrounded by townspeople listening eagerly to his, by now somewhat embellished, tales. Guess arriving a dragonback was impressionable.

It's a long flight back to the dwarves. A very long, boring flight. Turn to 201

285

The rocky outcrop that makes up the island is slippery. Even with your talons scraping against the algae-covered surface, it's all you can do to not fall into the waters. There's barely room to move and you have to press yourself against the stone wall of the castle to even fit on the tiny sliver of land available.

Stretching your long neck to the limit, you manage to get a glimpse over the outer wall. The insides of this grey fortress are as unforgiving as the outside and just as bleak. Everything is made from large blocks of grey stones and, despite all the staircases and levels, there are only a handful of darker slits in the facades and no doorways at all.

It takes everything you have, a furious amount of scratching and a tumble to get you over the outer wall. You hope it'll be easier getting out than it was getting in.

Testing one of the stone staircases with a paw, it feels solid enough. You have to squeeze yourself against the wall it follows to keep from falling off as you move upwards. Turn to 382

After a quick look around, you decide to head downwards. Turn to 242

286

The smell from tunnel one stings your nostrils. It's definitely not human.

If it's not human, you can definitely eat it — though if it tastes anything like what it smells, you're not sure you want to. Turn to 184

You decide to leave it alone and return to the cave just beyond the entrance to the mountain and the tunnel there instead. Turn to 170

287

This is simply not your day. Only one thing after another, and none of them in your favour. Did you insult someone you shouldn't have?

Maybe you'll have better luck with the third challenge? Turn to 193

You're going to have to admit defeat and return to the dwarves empty-handed. Dragons and Defeat do not mix. You roar your displeasure. Turn to 201

288

Rolling and frolicking around amongst the meadows, you can't imagine a better place for some rest and relaxation. Even the sky looks bluer from here.

Shaking off a bunch of petals, and tufts of grass, and clods of earth, you stretch and yawn. There. You smell so much better, you think. Now all you need is a small nap and you'll feel energised and ready to take on your next challenge.

Hopefully nothing will interrupt your snooze. All dragons hate having their "me" time disturbed. Turn to **148**

An alarm would come in handy, you think, as you curl up nose to tail. You just have to hope you wake up before dark. Turn to **197**

289

Dipping a wing, you bank leisurely, looking for a good landing spot. But the closer you get to the castle, the stronger your frills quiver. When even your bones are vibrating, threatening to shake your fangs from your jaw, you break off your approach. Blast it!

No damn castle is going to beat you. You circle around and try again. Turn to **154**

Snorting loudly, you shake your frills, trying to get the feeling back into them. What is going on here? You head towards the shore instead. Turn to **367**

290

It flashes again. Intrigued, you approach, sliding slightly on the treacherous sand.

It's a small bottle. Well, to a human it would be huge, you expect. It's easily the size of three grown men standing side by side. But in your hands it feels small.

You pick it up and bring it up to your eyes. It seems empty. You shake it and almost drop it when a string of expletives emanate from within.

You don't mean to pull out the plug. But it flies out of the bottle all on its own.
*Turn to **271***

291

Someone once told you that a wise man does not keep a dragon waiting. Apparently, this doesn't apply to wizards. Or maybe it does apply and you shouldn't keep a wizard waiting, either. Maybe the two cancel each other out? Either way, you lay down, grumbling to yourself.

Eventually the Archmage arrives — together with several others. They don't stay, though, merely drop the gear they were hauling up the mountain and leave.

In fact, the mountain top is a pretty desolate place now that you take the time to look around. There aren't even any eagles in sight.

Shaking his head when you share that you didn't, in fact, gather all the ingredients he asked you for, Kaheiron sighs deeply.

'We will not be needing all of this then,' he says.

'We won't? Why not? You mean I can't go home?'

'Of course you can return home. That was, in fact, the easy part — once we managed to isolate what that crazy old coot had done and work out how to reverse it,' the Archmage almost snorts. 'I was, however, hoping to offer you some alternatives, but it would appear we will have to do this in a more old-fashioned way.'

Not sure you like the sound of that, you have flashbacks to ideas of getting your skin torn off and a new form appearing below it. You take a few steps away from the black-haired Kaheiron. He hadn't struck you as the sadistic type, but appearances can be deceptive, you know that.

'Never fear, you'll return home safely and in your normal, human guise. I can not, however, guarantee, that the journey will be a comfortable or painless one,' Kaheiron says. He gives a curt nod as he pulls out a small pouch and pour some of the shimmering crystals into his hand.

'But … wait … what about …'

Your voice is cut off as you're tossed into a maelstrom of colours and shifting perspectives. Tumbling through the eather, you spare a thought for the companions you made on your journey, realizing that you'll probably never see them again.

292

Picking up the, only slightly squashed, creatures, you wing your way back to camp somewhat unsteadily. It's not as easy carrying carcasses in your claws as you would have thought.

You then find yet another positive to adventuring as a dragon. There's no trouble getting the fire started.

Also turns out roast meat taste better than raw, even to your new dragon palet. The smells wafting up from the cooking fire that you manage to get going (and you only set fire to two bushes in the process) are enough to make you salivate in anticipation.

*There are only two of them, but, after feasting, you feel like you've eaten several month's worth of food. Turn to **246***

293

What little remains of the house goes up in flame, whatever was hiding under all the rubble burned alive.

*Snorting some of the resulting smoke, you decide that this is getting boring. You want something bigger to put your teeth into. Turn to **332***

Cat companion: *Chaos watches, eyes as large as saucers. Before you have a chance to test if magical cat hairs burn too, he's leapt down from your shoulders and disappeared. Turn to **407***

294

After some digging and scraping at the solidified lava, you recover the biggest crystal you've ever seen. It's nearly the size of your right paw, but, while the light dances off it as you hold it this way then that, it's not what you're looking for.

*If you still have the satchel that the Archmage gifted you, you put the crystal in there for safe keeping. Turn to **390***

*You didn't come for shiny trinkets, but, looking about, you can't think of anything else that you might find here. Turn **151***

295

Gambling on the sage's advice, you turn your nose into the wind and change direction. Trouble is, all the landmarks he provided you with were, well, on land. Turns out they're nearly impossible to spot from the air. Reluctantly, you land at the edge of a small, and rather gnarly, forest.

With the stubbornness of dwarves and dragons, you keep ploughing ahead. It's got to be around here, surely?

After passing through an area where all the leaves have been stripped, leaving only bare, grey trunks, you come upon a small glade. You say small, but it easily accommodates both you and its, ahem, current occupant. You can't quite make out what's living in the glade, but they're not moving.

*Drawing back your shoulders and tightening your ribs, just in case, you decide to investigate. Turn to **328***

*Snorting, you huff. You should have known better than to follow the advice of some strange mortal. Turn to **364***

296

The battle is short.

You actually only meant to intimidate them a little, but when you attack, the dwarves retaliate with full force and without mercy. They know they can't win a protracted battle with a dragon, so they fall upon you with everything they have.

There are a lot of them and many of them are armed with weapons that will draw blood even from the likes of you. To say nothing about what the heavy machinery, which rolls out on well-oiled tracks from openings in the mountain, does.

You fight hard, and take many of them with you, but in the end, there is nothing for you here but painful death of a thousand stabs …

297

Grabbing the bottle, you're suddenly filled with the overwhelming desire to throw it all over yourself.

You don't feel any different afterwards. Then you catch your reflection in a mirror on the other wall and leap several feet into the air. Oh no!

What stares back at you is a dragon. A pink dragon. With purple spots and large eyeglass markings around your eyes.

Well, at least you can still bite anyone who laughs at you, you think as you leave the tower. Turn to **219**

There's only one potion you haven't tried now. If you're feeling lucky, this might be it. Turn to **187**

298

As their dying cry echoes pleasantly in your ears, something dark falls upon you from the sky. You turn just in time to growl menacingly, but the other dragon pays no attention to your antics. With a sweep of its paws, it knocks you aside, sending you tumbling over and over.

You hear something break followed by a searing pain in your wings. Looking up, you gaze into the furious eyes of a mature dragon of immense stature and power. You can't hold it. It's too powerful. You look away.

*Rearing, the other dragon, a creature black as midnight ink, craggy of feature and fleet of wing, throws back its head and blasts you with a searing light. Turn to **359***

299

It takes several days of doing nothing but flapping your wings (what is it with all this distance? Why couldn't they have arranged for everything to be much closer at hand?) to get near your target.

Strong puffs of wind are being disagreeable and constantly try to blow you off course, so you're pleased when, finally, you spot a wisp of smoke on the horizon. After that, it's not too long before you also catch sight of the volcano itself. Mt Snag is standing proud and tall, like a perfect cone, in the middle of an extended field of black rock that must once have been lava.

*The smoke isn't actually coming from the caldera itself, but several vents along the northern slope, so you decide to land right at the top, as benefits a king of the sky. Turn to **204***

*Not keen on getting your sensitive snout, or worse, your wing membranes, splashed with erupting magma, you decide to try the slopes first. Maybe you'll be lucky. Turn to **313***

300

As you curl up for the night, you keep wondering what you lost today. Not even sleep lets you off the hook. You spend the night getting chased by an overlarge leather bag with a soft mouth where the flap should have been. It hops after you. Hop. Hop. Hop. No matter how fast you run — it's right behind you.

Hop! Hop! HOP!

When you wake up the next morning you yawn and stretch. There's a terrible crick in your neck. Apparently, all those armoured scales only protect you from the outside. You must have pulled a muscle while asleep, trying to escape the Bag of Doom.

Now, what about breakfast? They still serve that here, right? Turn to **341**

Chaos looks at you and meows. Glancing down, you can see a dead mouse at the cat's paws. Narrowing your eyes, it looks like an awfully small meal for one. The grey cat hisses. Guess the mouse isn't a gift, but your companion's breakfast. Turn to **200**

301

The young man immediately launches into his tale — making you wonder if he's rehearsed it beforehand.

'Now, you must know, I was once a great warrior …'

This is a statement at which you snort a great amount of smoke, causing the young man to cough and look a little uncomfortable,

'Ahem … Yes … You see … I must prove my worth. The fair princess Eloneora was taken from her chambers in the night by a great brute not four days hence. Four times I have faced this monster. Four times I have failed to slay it. Perhaps you can do so in my stead? Surely nothing could threaten such a great beast such as yourself?'

He'd probably have had better luck at any rescuing if he hadn't left home in his Sunday best, you think, but you eventually agree to help him. Turn to **406**

Now, if you were to do him this great favour, what's in it for you, you want to know. Turn to **329**

302

Turning this way, then that, you gaze upon your reflection in mild awe. Your talons are nicely curved. Your wings, which you stretch experimentally, are graced with elegance as is the long, sinuous neck crested with pale armour plating. Your chest, rising and falling with each of your breaths, is deep and you can feel the beating of the powerful heart residing deep inside.

You look like you should weigh several tons, but you feel light on your feet. Every turn nimble; every swoosh of your long tail strong and agile. If elves were dragons, they'd be you.

Turning your graceful snout into the wind, you sniff a couple of times. There's something interesting coming from ... over there. Turn to **213**

Now that you're familiar with yourself, you just need to find out where you are. Maybe there's someone around to ask? Turn to **205**

303

A fleeing dragon doesn't make the most elegant of sights, but they do move fast. You're soon far from the garden.

Try to circle back and see if you can find that knight again. Turn to **324**

304

When you land, carefully as to not send the dwarves that have come out to watch, flying, and pull out the reagent, you're almost deafened by the cheers and shouts of joy. Several of the dwarves are tossing their helmets into the air. Big, warm, tears of joy roll down many a cheek, disappearing into the bushy beards below.

You come to understand that they'll be able to keep the forge going for centuries with this, but first they'll need to restart it. Turn to **247**

305

Beating your wings industriously, you soon zig and zag between and above tall, rocky hills and mountains so dry it's a wonder they don't crumble to the touch. Exploring in a matter of hours what would have taken a mortal man days, if not weeks, you eventually land on a likely looking outcropping.

The mountain slope here is quite steep, and your landing sets off a small avalanche of yellow and red stones. The echo when they eventually hit the bottom almost knocks you off your feet. That's a long way down.

To the left there is little to tell. Not even a trail. Good, that means people don't often come that way. That'll suit you just fine. Turn to **361**

Now that you're this close by, you can tell there's the mearest hint of a path — as if someone, or something, has gone through a great deal of trouble of concealing it — you can't really tell it's there unless you look at it from just the right angle. That could be troublesome. Best you find out before you decide if you want to hide anything here. Turn to **129**

306

Blinking in the bright light of day, the colours appear to drain from the world around you. Was your sacrifice truly worth it? Was the price to pay too high? You don't know. Maybe.

Everything seem different than you expected it. Colder. The clouds around you are moving in. Billowing cumulus, filled with lightning and thunder the clouds appear alight, as if by blue fire.

You barely notice ... so intent are you upon your internal struggle. Turn to **359**

307

Taking on something akin to a lava dragon, even a young one, in its own lair, is little more than a recipe for disaster. Your scales almost melt from the heat even as its first strike misses you, plunging straight into the wall of the caldera instead.

If you're a red dragon: Your blood-red scales quiver in the heat, almost aglow themselves. A few more moments of this and you'll burn up. Turn to **128**

It must have a weakness, somewhere, surely? You scan for it, increasingly desperate. Turn to **115**

Whatever happens, you're not going down without a fight. Turn to **122**

308

With equal amounts of gliding, jumping, and scrabbling on the rocks for what purchase you can find, you manage to reach a large shelf just above the lava lake. Gazing upwards, you realize that you've descended further than you'd thought. The sky is little but a blue circle right above, with walls closing in around you. Good thing you're not claustrophobic, right?

The lake occasionally glops, sending up bubbles of gas that makes you wrinkle your whole snout in disgust whenever they burst. You've never dared go this close to a volcano, a live volcano, before. Even through your draconic scales you can feel the heat trying to drown you. You amuse yourself by knocking over some loose rocks and send them tumbling into the lake. The smaller disappear with a puff before they even reach the glowing lava.

Only thing is, there's still no trace of the reagent you came here to find. And unless you're up for tearing the volcano apart with nothing but your strength going for you, the only place left to look is in the lake itself.

You bunch up, muscles quivering, and launch yourself into the pool of melted rock. Turn to **189**

For what was supposed to be a rich environment, there's hardly a trace of a reagent in sight. You decide to head back up. Turn to **348**

You can't help but stare at the wide, long-since-healed, scar running across the gryphon's leonine flank. It stands out sharply against the surrounding apricot fur and disappears underneath a bundle of milky white and grey feathers. You wonder what could have caused it when you feel their steely gaze upon you.

The gryphon warbles, tufted ears turning towards the Archmage, who nods and smiles knowingly, as if the two just shared a joke.

Your ears … do you *have* ears? You forgot to look. If you do, they flatten, your lip curling ever so slightly. No one likes being made fun of.

Now, the tufted ears of the gryphon rise in response and you're now being given their undivided attention. Looking into those swirling, amber eyes you have to stop yourself from taking a step backwards.

The gryphon splays their wings, giving you an unimpeded view of ochre, white, and red feathers. But what catches your eye are several black and blue feathers at the tip of their right wing. *Only* on their right wing. Those can't be natural, you think.

'Her name is Lightwing, and let me assure you, she understands you a lot better than you understand her,' Kaheiron says.

The gryphon squawks shrilly, as if to say, 'Yes, that's me. You've got a problem with that?'

The Archmage then provides you with a dragon-sized satchel packed with supplies. You're hoping it'll contain something to eat.

'Dragons tend not to eat often, but when you do grow hungry, you'll find that it requires sizeable portions to sustain you,' Kaheiron tells you as he sends you on your way.

You're hungry already, but eating the spellslinger probably isn't a good idea, so instead you follow your new companion into the sky. Turn to **123**

You watch the gryphon soar above you, swooping and diving — as if inviting you to play. But you doggedly keep on walking. Turn to **179**

310

Soon the dark specks turn into a whole flock … gaggle … pride … you're not sure … of gryphons. The graceful and agile flyers angle over the battlefield at a great height, in case anyone below decides to do something foolish.

Many sport dark tufts on their ears, their leonine hindquarters different shades of tawny, from almost white to so dark you'd almost call it black. Here and there you spot iridescent feathers among the brown and grey and white. To you, they seem to ignore you completely, flying steady and true towards their goal.

Gryphon companion: Lightwing calls out to the new arrivals who warble back. They almost sound like they're laughing as they split around you, speed past, and are gone before you know it. Lightwing is well ahead of you now, she seem to want you to follow her. You hope all the effort in following them isn't going to end up being for Aunty Lucy's special day out or something. Turn to 193

Actually, a nice snooze right about now would hit the right spot. Turn to 217

311

A caravan. And you thought this place was empty. How foolish. And if they're carrying freight, then, by definition, it should be valuable. And everything valuable belongs to you.

You touch down heavily right before them, sending many of the pack animals into a panic. Pleased with their reaction, you flare your wings and spit some fire. That should impress them. Oh, look, it did. They're running.

You snake around the frightened animals, purring happily, as you relieve them of their cargo, their sanity, and their lives.

There's a flash of light in the corner of your eyes. Someone's dropped something. Turn to 290

You're now far away from prying eyes. No one comes here if they don't have

312

You let out a mighty roar and leap forward, jaws agape.

Landing amongst the rubble, you flick the torn remains of a stone wall their way. The figures disappear for but a moment only to reappear where you least expected it.

They keep doing that. Every time you think you have them pinned down, they move. These aren't ordinary mercenaries at all. Your eyes narrow as you try to penetrate the stone.

Cloaks of Concealment. Hidden weapons. Magic arrows. Ouch! There goes another one. Right in your paw this time. All you need now is for one of them to have a magic sword and you're … OUCH!

You howl in pain. Whipping around reveals you've lost several feet of tail.

No. No. This isn't how it's supposed to be. You're not supposed to run into a band of bloody heroes. It's not fair.

*Well, that does it. You rumble menacingly. You need to gather your strength. They're just a bunch of losers. You can do this. It's easy. They're ants. Nothing but puny ants. Turn to **349***

313

The rock you land on is solidified lava and it's covered in a fine layer of black dust. Landing on it, you fire off three huge sneezes in a row when it swirls up around you. The particles are abrasive and scratch your throat when you breathe them in. You have to raise your head high to get some fresh air.

*Everything around you looks pretty much the same. Grey and dreary. Hunting for anything here looks to you like a lost cause. Turn to **171***

Cat companion: *Chaos isn't at all pleased with trying to breathe powdered*

314

Who knew trees could be this boring? They all look alike to you. Their friends
and family might be able to tell them apart, but to you they only look like so
much kindling.

*Shaking your behorned head at the folly of it all, you wonder what you are
doing out here anyway? Turn to **287***

*What's that? Something moved, just there. Didn't it? Turn to **227***

315

In fact, as you swim downwards, the world keeps growing larger and, even
stranger, brighter. It's not long until everything around you is coming up a
tropical azure and you can see for what feels like miles.

Of course, *you* can see for miles any day, now, but not even your eyes have
been able to penetrate the murky waters of the lake before. Now, everything
around you is teeming with life. As you move closer, you see large, towering
structures growing from the sandy bottom. They remind you a bit of termite
mounds but made of sand and crystal and glass. Around them, a myriad of
inhabitants are going about their daily business.

When they see you, they blow bubbles at you.

Everything around you seems to be emitting some form of light. Glowing
fishes are hitched to underwater chariots. Shrimp-like people, their fins flowing like angel hair, are a pale white. What you guess are pets gambol around
in an array of colours: blue and green and grey and purple.

*But you can't stay to see more. You have a castle to get to. You swim on. Turn
to **285***

The great wyrms of the sea need to breathe only every few hundred years, but you're a dragon and, right now, a tiny one at that. You can only hold your breath for that long. You have no choice but to return to the surface. Turn to **383**

316

Your companion meows at you, batting one paw against your scales. Chaos seems confident about his place on your shoulders, you think. Is he? Yes, he is. He's actually washing his face right there, in the air. What does he think you are, a taxi service?

Grinning, you test your balance with a few winged antics then, when that doesn't earn a protest, you execute a barrel roll. Your companion yowls but clings on, sharp claws digging into scales strong enough to withstand harpoons.

Unfortunately, the leather satchel that the Archmage provided you with doesn't have such abilities. Down and down it goes. Falling.

You dive after it, but it disappears with a splash in the lake far below. Roaring in frustration, you pull up just as you're about to hit the water, throwing up a huge wave in your wake. Your companion merely sits back down, giving you one of those, 'I told you so,' looks that all cats are famous for.

Guess you'll never know what was in that satchel now. You hope there wasn't any food, because it looks like dinner will be lacking tonight, as, after many hours, you return to the ground. Turn to **300**

Twilight eventually descends, but you're not the least bit tired. It feels like you could do this for ages. Why stop now? Wings beat the air, the wind, and you decide to just keep flying through the night. Turn to **200**

317

Slowing down your approach and watching the next two gryphons carefully, you follow their lead. Climbing high, tucking your wings in tight, so tight, and then dive. The wind whistles in your ears.

The hole is coming up fast, now. At the last moment, fear grabs you and you screw your eyes shut.

Then, glorious freedom.

Yee-haw!

You did it. Your wings snap open and you do a victory roll, your dragonform a sharp darkness against the bright blue sky. Turn to **183**

318

Soon there are tables, a chair, and lots of plates covered by cakes of every kind — all sending tingling feelings to your nostrils and stomach both. There's also a large water pitcher and what looks like an old beer barrel.

'That's for you,' the princess points to the barrel. 'I'm sorry you had to run into Richar. He really is the biggest nuisance. Ever since Dearhundt had that accident, mixing spells and all that, he's been after him … and me.'

Dearhundt lumbers into view, carrying the largest platter filled with fruit and vegetables that you've ever seen. You're not sure if to be appalled or curious. While walking upright and on two legs, everything else about him is a mismatch of animal parts — so many you doubt you'd be able to name them all.

You're expecting a deep, rumbling slur, so when the clipped, sharp tones of Dearhundt emerge, you're more than a little surprised.

Tea drunk and cakes eaten, the princess and Dearhundt give you some good directions to follow. Turn to **146**

You've heard enough. It's not your problem. Your belly is full and now you just want the gold. Turn to **389**

319

There's no tingling feeling when you dip a talon into the water. Nor does your paw turn heavy and try to drag you to the bottom, having turned to gold.

A little disappointing really, you think, and pull it up again. It's covered, absolutely covered, in a thin film of … something. Like a rock pulled from the water, it's already lost its glimmer.

Pulling up several bushes trying to rub it off, you finally give up. Hopefully it'll dry, flake and fall off on its own. In the meantime, you'll have a bright, yellow paw. You decide to go hunting to take your mind off it. Turn to **107**

320

Several of the other dragons bellow back. Damn it, did they just increase their speed? Two of the flanking flyers break off, banking left and right. What? Are they going to try and get behind you? How dare they?

No way you're going to get scared off by some scruffy, scaly twats. Anything they can do to you, you'll return tenfold. Turn to **397**

321

A little later, as you take a break, and take out your frustration on some innocent trees, your hearing picks up something interesting. You pad over, through the small copse, to find a rustic looking horse and cart. Two wheels have sunk deep down into a hole and the whole thing is now listing terribly.

The owner isn't anywhere in sight, but you do hear shouts coming from further away. You right the cart and frightened, neighing horse carefully and go on your way, no one the wiser.

Steeling yourself, every muscle tensing to breaking point, you gnash your teeth. Your hackles rise. You're going to beat this, darnit! Turn to **193**

You've always dreamed of having adventures in faraway lands. But this isn't quite what you had imagined it to be. Maybe going home while you're still in one piece wouldn't be such a bad idea after all? Turn to **172**

322

You keep walking and walking without, seemingly, ever getting anywhere. Then the tunnel begins to grow smaller. Soon it's too small to even fit your head into. You can't go any further. But there's something ahead. A light.

You growl, frustrated, and rake your claws across the stone walls. Realizing that it'll take you ages to dig through the hard stone, you let off a roar that travels like shockwaves in the narrow tunnels. The mountain trembles with your rage.

Cat companion: *Chaos is, against all odds, still with you. The pesky cat meows and dashes forward. Turn to* **103**

There's nothing to do but back up all the way until you're back where you started. Turn to **158**

323

It takes days, then you spot something glittering on the horizon. The closer you get, the more obvious it is that your dream of soft, white beaches and rolling in the sand will not be coming true any time soon. The shore is rocky and, to your eyes, quite barren.

Where the ocean doesn't lap at the stone, it churns against cliffs rising like straight towers out of the depths. There isn't a single fishing boat within your sight — and you strain your eyes to see them. But there are a lot of birds. Large, white birds cover the cliffs. In fact, until something moved, you thought the cliffs were white, there are that many.

It's a good thing you're a dragon, you think as you veer out over the sea.

There are some oddly behaving waves off to your left. Curious, you bank slowly to see it better. Turn to **164**

There is a dark speck on the horizon. It's the only land within miles and miles and it's calling your name. Turn to **124**

<h1 style="text-align:center">324</h1>

Approaching the knight you try to appear non-threatening. A feat no dragon is particularly well suited for without appearing silly — and you don't do silly — but, with the visor down, you're not sure he can see you anyway. He also seems to have sunk down into the grass up to his calves. Maybe the grass ate his horse too?

You poke the knight to see if he's still alive. Turn to **102**

An empty suit of armour isn't going to be of any use to you so, snorting a bit of flame in annoyance, you stalk off. There's still a reagent to find. Turn to **314**

<h1 style="text-align:center">325</h1>

Gathering everything up, even the large sack feels small in your claws. You need to hold it carefully, lest you pierce it and spill those precious, glittering gold coins across the lands beneath you. You have no interest in making anyone else rich. That privilege is yours and yours alone. All treasure should belong to you.

You sniff the air after a day or so. You can smell it. It's faint, but the promise of precious metal comes from somewhere below. You arch your sails, slowing you down, and begin a circling pattern, scanning for what might give off such deliciousness.

Then you spot them. It's a rider leading two heavily laden pack horses. He's wearing a bright tunic and what he probably thinks is a jaunty cap. A tax inspector.

Old bile begins to rise in your throat. Faint memories of intense dislike only grows stronger when fed through your draconic heart. NO! ALL the monies are yours!

Diving down, you toss him into the air. His screams are cut off as he disappears down your gullet.

The packhorses bolted at the sight of you, but you run them down easily.

You're not sure why you're hungry all the time, you're certain dragons aren't supposed to eat this much, but as you separate them from what gold they carry you also separate them from their lives. Then, sated and rested, you turn your snout to new lands. Turn to **332**

326

One swing from the erratically moving broom shoves the whole end into one of your nostrils, cobwebs and all. You give one mighty sneeze, making a fireball twice the size of the cave entrance roll across the garden.

Whoops! You didn't mean to do that. Apologize profusely to try and make up for it. Turn to **134**

Don't bother to apologize but instead snatch the princess. Turn to **389**

327

Clutching your rock tightly, you watch. The gryphons are quite masterful but there are dirty glances thrown your way by those that have already dropped their weapons — for that must be what the rocks are: Weapons.

You think the stupid fish should just return to the depths, where it won't get pelted by gryphon rocks, but it keeps thrashing and snapping until, eventually, the onslaught becomes too much.

And you still haven't made your run.

Too late now.

Disappointment burns through your veins. That should have been you. *You were supposed to get the credit and the glory. Turn to* **244**

You're not impressing anyone, least of all the gryphons present. Turn to **172**

328

On closer inspection, it turns out that what you thought was a living thing is actually a block of ice. Except this ice isn't melting. Must be some sort of crystal then, you guess. It's not quite clear and you can just see a hint of a shape inside.

It's definitely not moving and you knock against the crystal with a talon. It echoes back, as if what's inside is much further away than a few feet of crystalline rock.

Maybe if you try to bite it?

A moment later, you spit out a tooth. Great. Now your teeth ache. So much for that idea.

Maybe picking it up and dropping it from a great height, like an eagle and a tortoise, will shatter it? Turn to 231

When all else fails, ask nicely, someone once told you. You can't see how that'd help — it's not like the crystal has ears. But you try anyway. Turn to 109

329

The young man must have realized your reluctance when you begin to examine bits and pieces of his gear for treasures and trinkets.

The pouch of gold and silver coins he offers you don't smell a lot like either gold nor silver to your sensitive nose, but the money will come in handy.

Accepting the payment, you start off in the direction the man points. Turn to 406

330

It's not heavy, but the ocean pulls at your wings as they splash down into the water again and again as you try and catch something no larger than a couple of big, round cheeses. It could have been a lot easier, but you struggle to make sure you don't harm it.

You're nearly pulled under a couple of times, but finally your talons enclose the small, bedraggled piece of fluff and you can bring it back to the island from which you're pretty sure it came.

A guess confirmed as right when you're mobbed by a whole host of grateful and happy gryphons as you land.

You wish they weren't quite *as friendly actually ... even scales are no match for a thankful nip from those powerful beaks. Turn to* **270**

331

Several months later, when you have conveniently forgotten the Archmage's warnings, exactly what he warned you about comes to pass. You explode! Go directly to the afterlife. Do not pass to the next world. Do not collect two-hundred doubloons.

332

You soar in the increasingly cloudless sky for hours upon hours. Beneath you there is sand. Nothing but sand. And maybe a few cracked rocks poking out of the hot sea. You pass what might once have been riverbeds filled with the lifeblood of the desert, now dusty, dirty snakes winding their way into nothing.

There are no buildings you can see. No structures of any kind. When you eventually do spot what you think is an oasis on a horizon that shimmers and shifts with the suns, you head straight for it. It's the only exciting thing you've found out here so far.

You only slow down enough to drop your burden, if you still have it, beyond the palm trees, then plunge straight into the water. Turn to **252**

Despite the place so obviously being abandoned to your eyes, you land a little beyond the oasis, choosing to walk the rest of the way. Turn to **223**

333

You pull up just in time as the maws of an anglerfish's evil, and much bigger, cousin, snap shut, swallowing what feels like half the sea along with it. That thing was a monster. Beady eyes watch you, the prey that escaped, as it slowly sinks back down into the dark waters.

A little unsteady on your wings, you head straight for the remote island after that. Turn to **270**

334

Your head snakes out, fast as lightning, but before your jaws snap shut around the furry feline he disappears in a poof.

You throw back your head and roar in anger. Turn to **392**

335

When you find it, the waters are clearer than any you've ever seen. And while the river might have seemed deep and wide to a human, to a dragon it's nothing but a few leaps and bounds.

You accidentally knock over some rocks by the bank and watch them sink with a splash. It takes some time before they hit the rocky bottom, drifting away slightly even at their weight. Looks like there's a fast current along the bottom.

Looking down, you spot several silvery shadows. Good. You could do with a nice fish dinner. They dart away as you hit the water's surface with your paw, the water you do scoop up draining through scaled digits.

It takes a few more tries, but soon you've gathered quite the pile. But, while your human mind insists that a whole stack of rainbow-trout is more than enough, your draconic tummy begs to differ.

*Well, that could have gone better. Guess fish isn't very filling when you're a dragon. Turn to **200***

*Looks like you're going to have to find sustenance elsewhere, you think. You did spot a faint trail of smoke rising earlier. Maybe there's a settlement nearby? Turn to **182***

336

Roars, hisses, snarls, and heavy thumps as if limbs strike the earth are all enveloped and drowned out by the thunder that is the great tree crashing down, roots tipping into the air. You've uprooted the ironwood's stronger cousin successfully.

But your success is short-lived when, shooting out from between broken branches, the wyrm sinks its fangs into your left leg. Even while tearing it off, stomping on its body, your sighs begins to fill with darkness. Those fangs were poisonous after all. Your body thrashes violently as froth flies from your mouth and the pained darkness claims you.

337

Today isn't proving to be one of your better days. Guess even dragons have them. Flying always seems to calm you down, so you head up, above the clouds.

*Feeling increasingly like you just want to stomp on the whole world, you keep flying. Turn to **332***

*Flying isn't as soothing as usual, but, slowly, the feeling of wanting to burn the entire world dissipates. Slowly. Turn to **321***

338

It's not long before the roughly hewn walls of the tunnel grow into intricate carvings. Niches, even the occasional ornamental pillar, begin to appear. Sometimes the space in between them is glowing, ever so faintly.

The light in the niches isn't still but wavers, like waves lapping the shore, swirling slowly. Could they be doorways? Hidden portals to some long dead sorcerer's secret lair? Turn to **359**

Ignoring the glowing niches, you keep going until it feels like you've walked all the way to the other side of the mountain. Turn to **234**

339

You dive through the last cloud layer. The smell that wafts up on the warm, rising air almost makes you gag.

Telling your stomach to behave, you scan what once must have been verdant fields. Turn to **106**

You hear the sounds of battle drifting up from further ahead and, curious, you climb a bit to get a better look. Turn to **256**

340

Consulting your map, the next challenge appears to lie somewhat further inland. Not sure what scale the map is to, or even if it's to scale at all, you can't tell how far it is without first identifying the most prominent landmarks. It can't be too far, you think later, as you scan the world beneath you with keen eyes. Dragons can be mighty swift flyers when they want to be. But you've flown for what feels like hours and haven't stumbled (or flown into) a single, outstanding feature yet.

You might not be able to hold a map in the air, but dipping down once in a while below the clouds, you finally recognize several of the landmarks that the Archmage showed you in a shower of magical sparks. You're getting closer. Also, you figure that a big, bloody mountain is hard to miss.

*There seems to be an awful lot of mountains to choose from, including one the summit of which reminds you a little bit of an eagle. Turn to **358***

*Perhaps you should take your chances on a more inconspicuous looking mountain? Turn to **209***

341

You draw in a deep breath. Your sensitive nostrils fill with scents from a myriad of things you never even knew were there before. A gazillion different leaves, all with their own aroma.

Trees, the bark of one which tingles at the back of your throat, musky and deep. There are flowers, the smell of warm air and dry vegetation. Insects and animals. From tiny mice to lumbering oxen — you can smell them all. The last lands right on your taste buds, bypassing your brain and assaults your stomach, which rumbles in reply.

Is this how the world really smells? Wow. Your puny human nose sure came up short in comparison.

Letting out a loud, 'harrumph,' your stomach tightens yet again. Rummaging through the satchel, it contains plenty of strange supplies, but not much that looks edible and certainly not big enough to sustain a dragon's appetite.

*You can smell running water in the wind. There's a large river not too far from where you are and rivers all have fish, right? Turn to **335***

*Most scents you can't discern what they are, but you figure the heavy, musky undertones should belong to something big. A plump deer should settle you nicely. You just need to catch it first. Turn to **276***

342

After several hours of non-stop flying, you come upon a large, circular lake. In the middle of the lake, there is a small island and upon that island there stands a castle. It looks pretty forbidding for a castle. More of a fortress, really, with high grey walls of stone rising from the water's surface. It seems to suck all the brightness out of the surrounding area. All life. The Castle of Stone. And within it lies your first challenge.

Swinging around, you try to land directly at the castle. Turn to **289**

The place doesn't just look like it would turn lesser adventurers into a small smudge of fear but give them second and third ideas about approaching. Not you, of course, but you decide to land on the far shore even so. Turn to **367**

343

'No? Not to your liking? I can make you wish you'd never disturbed my slumber.' The Djinn snaps his finger again.

All of a sudden you feel something nibbling at you. Rats. Tens, hundreds, no, thousands of rats and mice and gerbils are crunching their way to your centre. You're made of cake. Dry, stale, cake.

'Stop This!' You bellow. You try to shake them off, only dropping crumbs everywhere.

'Not what you wished for? Very well. Then, how about this?' The Djinn snaps his fingers and with a flash you're big again. And a dragon. And not made out of cake. Turn to **278**

The Djinn merely laughs, again. A laugh totally devoid of merry. He snaps his fingers and you blink out of existence and time. Turn to **290**

344

You manage to get a good grip on the sword and, with a mighty heave, or two, or three, it grudgingly slides out of its wooden prison. Now that you can look at it closer, it looks like it's been stuck in the tree for quite some time. Certainly longer than the knight has been here.

Shrugging your impressive shoulders, you hand the sword over to the knight, who can barely avoid squealing with glee as he takes it.

A moment later and he has stabbed you in the heart with it.

It must have been a magical sword, for it cuts through scales and spines and bones alike.

'Take that, foul creature!' is the last you hear as you drift from this world.

345

You turn around as something small, grey, and furry leaps onto your bed, sits down, tail draped over their front paws, looks at you and meows expectantly. 'Chaos!' you exclaim happily.

346

Folding your wings, you dive towards the herd on the plain. The wind is whistling in your ears, your wings quivering as your heart beats rapidly.

It's going a little faster than expected and you overshoot the herd. Banking hard, you circle back after the now running, braying animals. All their hooves together roll over the plain like thunder. They're fast. Much faster than you thought — but not as fast as a dragon.

Coming in for a second attempt, you try to slow down. Flaring your wings, claws extended, you attempt to pluck a nice, juicy, fat one but misjudge the distance.

CRASH!

Instead of soaring into the sky with your prey like a triumphant eagle, you plough into the ground, scattering clods of earth far and wide. Alas, not all is lost. It looks like you landed on a few of your prey.

They're a bit squashed, but as you bite into the soft flesh, their juices run down your chin, tasting far better than you'd ever have imagined. Turn to **353**

Looking down, they don't look so big now. Kind of scrawny even. You don't fancy eating them raw, so decide to bring them back to camp. Turn to **292**

347

You're jolted awake as if someone had just run several thousand volts through your system … repeatedly. Awake but more than a little dazed, the world is swimming before your eyes. So sleepy. Your head, which has been slowly sinking back onto the ground, jerks up as, again, something almost electrical stings you.

'Good, you're awake,' rumbles a voice and, what you thought was night, moves.

'What?' You ask, trying to blink away the layer of dust and dirt on your eyes. You're confronted with the view of a large and very craggy, black dragon.

'This is not a good place to sleep,' the other dragon says. He, you assume it's a he, points at several nearby mounds. 'They fell asleep here, never to wake again.'

'WHAT?' You shoot up, realize that you're covered with dust and spores, and begin a wild dance trying to wipe it all off.

The other dragon merely shakes his head solemnly. 'I believe I was quite particular about when and where we should meet again. Everything was pre-pared, but as you deigned not to show, I'm afraid I can no longer offer you a choice in the matter of your return to your own world.'

'You can't?' Your eyes grow wide as the other dragon nods. 'What'you mean you can't?'

Features like a lost lava field after a drought move into what seems a cross between a frown and a grin as the black dragon shakes his behorned head again. Then you remember, Kaheiron had said he was an Archmage. It must all be an illusion then.

'Of course not,' the black dragon snorts. 'This is my natural form. And yes, I'm afraid that we will have to do this the hard way. You took so long in arriving that the potion has congealed, so we will have to scatter it as particles. Now, if you can remain still …'

As Kaheiron is pulling out a handful of liquid crystals, you take a step backwards, your tail squashing the flowers and grass at each swish. 'Now … wait a minute …' you exclaim.

'No time,' Kaheiron says, toss the crystals over you and starts muttering under his breath.

You're not sure what's supposed to happen and, for a brief moment, nothing does. Then the entire world snaps like a rubber band and you're pulled into the space between worlds, into where the mere potentiality of existence courses through the eather, and back towards your own world.

348

As you turn, beginning your climb back up, the pool below gurgles and glops. Is it your imagination or is it making more noises than before? Thanks to your long neck, you maintain your precarious purchase on the rocks and turn to see what's going on.

As you watch, what first looks to be rocks, float to the surface. Two large, bulbous eyes, appear in the craggy stone as the lava slowly drips off, then two more, further down. Oh no, something does live down here. And it doesn't look happy.

Lava cascading down its rocky hide, the young coulee rises slowly from the viscous lake, unfolding its stone encrusted wings until it nearly blots out the sun.

This would be a good time to climb a little faster, you think, and increase your upward speed. Turn to **370**

Growl menacingly yourself and turn to face the coulee. Turn to **307**

Gryphon companion: *Where the blazers is your feathered companion when you need them? You call out to Lightwing for help. Turn to* **261**

349

You catch a whiff of their scents. No. They're not all human. Blast. A sole human party is much easier to deal with, even when they are armed with magic weapons.

Bam!

Something explodes above you. You flinch, missing a step. Something else, something small and nimble dashes across the ground below. Before you can flick it away, it stings your paw with its slender sword.

Another tries to stab you in the eye. Leaping down from above. No! No! You need to get out of here. Dragonscales can only protect you from so much.

Something bites you, right on the snout. You see a flash of yellow. Stumbling backwards now, you're desperately looking for a way out. But they're manoeuvring you farther and farther back — your wings are scraping against rock walls now. You mean to blast them all with a bout of dragonfire but it flickers and dies, leaving behind nothing but the taste of dying embers and smoke.

There's only one way out. Forwards. But there you see, outlined against the dying light of the day, four figures. For but a moment, the scene is set — like a painting of old — then all hell breaks loose as you launch yourself upon them.

It's the last thing you'll ever do.

It's little comfort, had you known, that you'd live on in song and legend for centuries. That they'll decorate the new treasure chamber with images of your dying moments, as a warning to all thieves, should any dare to enter.

350

Exhausted dwarves finish piling your tribute on the large, very large, sack cloth sewn together in haste, with patches of sheepskin where worn thin. You frown at it. There's a lot less than you expected. You emit a low growl and watch the dwarves closest to you jump.

Oh, watch how they scurry about. You can't understand how such pitiful creatures could ever build anything, least of all an intricate civilization.

Now that you've gathered some more treasure, you decide to stash it along *with your previous spoils. Turn to **391***

*You take silver goblets, golden wreaths, candlesticks in ornamental bronze, and merely gilded iron along with things you don't even have a name for. Turn to **325***

351

A startled dragon is a little more than instincts and raw power. Before your magic runs out, everything in front of you has been scorched from the earth. Well, almost everything. The small, midnight blue, kobold — sans clothing — hasn't moved. He doesn't look hurt, but he sure doesn't look happy, either. Turns out kobolds are impervious to dragonfire … whoops.

*Red heat rises to your cheeks and you turn tail and escape as fast as you can. Turn to **196***

*Apologise profusely. Turn to **251***

352

Along with the gryphons you batter the huge sea creature with every rock in your arsenal. It's so big it's almost impossible to miss, but the smaller stones bounce off the slippery scales as if they were made out of rubber.

It snaps and churns the waters. Its tail creates waves a small barque would struggle to ride. The sail on its back wobbles, sending water flying through the air. Some of it splashes across your head.

The smell of fish assaults your nostrils. As you try to claw it out, the rock you're holding slips from your grasp. Down it goes … right into the monster's eye. The cry sends shivers through your very bones as the monster fish flicks its tail and disappears under the surface.

*From up on high, you see the shadow moving in the water. Turn to **207***

*You drag your tail in the water, like the gryphons earlier, to try and lure it back up. Turn to **244***

353

Rolling over, you manage to disentangle all limbs and, with the best draconic manners, gorge yourself on the fresh meat. There's no need for all that time-consuming cooking now. Great.

After the heavy meal, you curl up and fall asleep. Turn to **246**

354

The dwarves at Noame Mountain are mightily pleased to see you. So much so that they don't even haggle much over the price of a horse for the knight. It only costs him the magic sword. He doesn't look happy about it, you think.

But that might just have been the flight in. The knight had not been a good passenger, going distinctly green in the first minute and staying that way until several hours after you landed.

The dwarves haul the great tree away — presumably to turn it into some sort of kindling. Now you just have to start the forge — as soon as someone shows you how. Turn to **247**

355

Flapping hard, you carefully touch down by one of the wider roads. The dust you disturb on the dry dirt track sends you into a coughing fit, but once that's over, you trot over to what, from the sky, looked like a wooden shed with a garden growing on top of it. Turns out it is, in fact, made of stone. Long, rectangular stone blocks that imitates wood quite well, until you start tapping them with a claw.

So, the people here build things like these? Of stone? When there's enough ancient timber growing on the mountain to make any logger cry tears of joy? Yeah, that makes sense — not.

Leaning down, you peer closer at the small structure. Seems the door is made of metal and on it hangs the biggest padlock you've ever seen. It's still tiny compared to you, and you really need to crouch down to get a good look.

One thing's sure, you think. Whoever built these things, they sure didn't want to get robbed.

You can't see anyone around, but your neck scales and spines are quivering. Something, or someone, out there is watching you, you can feel it. Looks like it is ... a kobold? Turn to **147**

For a dragon, you're not very patient. If there's nothing around here, then you won't be here either. There's sure to be something more fun to do elsewhere. Turn to **236**

Wondering if the second challenge was a dud, you snort something about evil wizards and decide to throw all your chances in with the third challenge, if you can find it. Turn to **193**

356

Waiting for anything is agony, but when the footfalls are nearly upon you they stop. And still there is no sign of the walker. What are they? An invisible giant?

'Down here, you overgrown lizard!' comes from below. It's followed by a sharp rap that stings like lightning.

Down below, the smallest person you've ever seen, dressed in a smock of brown and green and gold, glares at you from behind a bushy beard. He's also hefting a big stick at you.

And you were actually afraid? How silly you feel. Turn to **238**

Somehow, below that tuft of hair, those eyes are actually pretty intimidating. Turn to **150**

357

You realize your useless companion has been yowling at you for some time and batting you with its tiny paws. Pesky critter. Doesn't it know how to shut up? It keeps up the tirade as you make short work of the two oxen — the farmer having fled — and the cow. You leave the goat, feeling very magnanimous about that.

*Trampling the newly sown fields, you survey the destruction around you. It's rather underwhelming, really. You want a bigger target. Something that burns for longer. Turn to **377***

358

Circling high in the sky, you can see fields of green and ripening crops creeping upwards from the foothills and many, smaller areas where people are growing … something … higher up. There are faint traces of dirt roads and even fainter tracks that can really only be spotted from above, all nestled in between alternatingly harsh and craggy looking peaks and the denser forests that cover nearly everything else.

*Speeding up, the wind soon races past as you fly away, the landscape blurring beneath you. Turn to **236***

*There's still no trace of the city you're supposed to find, though. You decide to circle lower and take your chances on the current mountain after all. Turn to **355***

359

As your snout comes in contact with the magical barrier, it sucks you in amongst a shower of sparks. For a moment you hang in the world between — suspended in everything and nothing.

The fury and rage almost consumes you, eating its way from the tip of your tail to the furthest point of your snout. Then the world flickers and goes cold.

When next you open your eyes, you're struck by how bright everything is. So bright you can't actually see anything. Then you realize that you're trying to stare right into the glowing bulb of a streetlight. You're so close to it that it's almost burning your face.

You're back in your own world. Looking down, you can see that you're still a dragon.

An evil grin spreads slowly over your dark features.

360

It's a long journey back, but eventually you catch sight of a rugged looking mountain up ahead. It rises above several of its kin, and, though you spot the occasional bush and weed further down, the top half of the mountain is completely devoid of anything but crags and rocks and gravel of every type you can imagine. Rather than coming to a point, the steep sides mellow out into an almost rolling spine.

You have no trouble locating the man you came here to see. Even if the robes and hair make him stand out in any crowd, he is, here, the only living thing that moves.

'Nice place,' you say and toss your head sarcastically.

'I would prefer not to accidentally shatter any living being in the vicinity should this not go quite according to plan,' the Archmage says. He throws the contents of another small pouch into the cauldron that stands in front of him.

'What?' You back up, startled. 'You mean I can STILL explode?'

'If this works, no.'

'I think I prefer this without the ifs,' you say and shudder.

'Did you successfully retrieve all the items I asked for?' Kaheiron asks and you notice, for the first time, that the cauldron is stirring itself. You hope you're not going to have to drink that, as you glance down at the thick, unappetising concoction.

'Of course,' you reply — affronted that he should even have to ask. Doesn't he think you know what you're doing? This might be a different world, but it isn't your first quest. Turn to **404**

Hanging your head you shake it and offer him the pieces you did *manage to retrieve. Turn to* **229**

361

After a great deal of trying to poke your snout into boring holes too small to fit a dragon, or even a malnourished dwarf, and turning over even duller rocks to find out if they might conceal an entrance into vast underground chambers, you eventually discover a jagged mouth leading into the mountain.

The top of your ridge spines scrape against the ceiling, showering you in gravel and dust, but you manage to squeeze inside.

Beyond the mouth there is a small antechamber with a floor worn almost smooth from years of wear. It's large enough that you can move freely, but your tail keeps knocking against the walls. It's a bit smaller than you had hoped for but there are two passages leading deeper into the mountain.

You take the smaller of the two passages. Turn to **142**

The larger passage looks, well, more passable, so that's where you try your luck first. You just hope there aren't any goblins down here. You'd hate to have to eat any. You don't imagine goblins taste very nice. Turn to **170**

362

Folding your wings neatly, as to avoid scraping everything around you and knocking over relatively, innocent squirrels, you creep towards the sound. Peering around a large bush, you see the racket is emanating from what looks to be a young man. Once dressed in what must have been finery, his clothes are in tatters and the fine gold thread from the embroidery hangs loose from the stained tunic.

He gives a small yelp when catching sight of you, fumbles with his sword, then sits back down heavily with a, 'woe betide me!' 'Woe, for what a magnificent dragon at whose claws I must now surely perish, never to again see my true love, she of the beauty beyond compare. The fair princess Eloneora. Woe betide me, for I shall be instead rendered asunder by this great beast who cares nothing for my troubles. Woe. Oh, woe.'

*Wrinkling your muzzle in disgust, you leave the young man to keep on berating his fate. Turn to **146***

*The idea of princesses peaks your interest and you decide to hear him out. Turn to **301***

*He really does go on rather a bit, you think. His voice alone grates on your ears. Isn't he a knight? Knights surely should be made of sterner stuff than that? Well, you can help by reducing their numbers a little, you decide and promptly squash him beneath your paw. Turn to **208***

363

'Hmm,' the Archmage studies what you have offered him. You have no idea what such diverse items would do if dropped in a potion, they're not exactly the kind of ingredients you'd have imagined one to be brewed from.

'This could will be interesting,' Kaheiron tells you. Though you notice he still picks up the items. He doesn't, however, induce any of them into the concoction that just went, 'glop,' as you watch it. You run your tongue over your sharp fangs. Even just watching it makes the taste fill your mouth and turn your stomach — or maybe that's the odour it's emitting.

'Not to fear, we have found the way to return you whence you came. It might, however, be somewhat of a bumpy ride. I'm quite certain that we've pinpointed your origin correctly. There might be some temporal shifts though. Nothing to worry about, I'm sure.'

Kaheiron smiles pleasantly at you as you feel your body beginning to fade from your existence in this strange new world. You didn't quite catch that last bit, but it sounded important.

*The vortex pulls and tugs at you. All you can do it hope whatever spells the mage has weaved will bring you back safely — and in the right shape. Turn to **229***

'Wait,' you call out. 'My friend. What about my companion!' You desperately cast your eyes around for them, but your loyal companion is nowhere to be seen. 'You won't even let me say goodbye you ba...' Turn to **186**

364

Feeling a touch foolish, and with an increasingly low opinion of those who inhabit this world, there's nothing for it but to gather up your wings and legs and find your own way.

This way looks interesting. It has mushrooms. Turn to **133**

No, you'd much rather spin fast, then head in whatever direction your snout points when you, somewhat dizzy, stop. Turn to **221**

365

First you growl. Then you rumble. Then you roar! Nothing. Apparently it'll take a bit more to get the attention of whomever lives here. You take a few deep breaths and let rip a roar so earth shattering that it shakes your very bones.

Answering booms come from the cave — or maybe they're just very heavy footsteps. Either way, you're not sticking around to find out. Turn to **146**

Crouching down, you're prepared to leap at anything that comes out of that cave. Turn to **108**

366

Arching his back, Chaos hisses. What he thinks of this little adventure is obvious and, looking around, you don't really feel like arguing. What a bleak looking place. And there's miles and miles of it, though at the borders all around there is a very lush, almost tropical, forest.

The only thing you want right now, though, is either a nice, ancient treasure a reagent, or a bath.

*In this, you spot something shiny in the distance and head over to investigate. Turn to **294***

*Stepping backwards, your right hind leg breaks the crust of an active lava tunnel, dropping you halfway into it. You manage to pull yourself up, but not before the flowing lava burns one of your wings. Turn to **151***

367

The shore is full of broken weeds and gnarly roots of trees long since forgotten, but it's not far and you soon land on a mixture of pebbles and flat, brown rocks protruding out into the lake.

Something in the bushes hisses at you. You lash out with your tail. There's a yelp followed by running footsteps. Whatever it was, it looks like you scared it away.

*Deciding you deserve a break after what you just went through, you wade into the shallow water. Spreading your wings wide, they let you float like a giant inflatable boat. Turn to **121***

*Finding a dinghy to ferry you across the water, gliding silently surrounded by an eerie glow, might work if you were still human-sized. Now, not so much. But if you can't reach the castle by air or boat, maybe you can swim there? Turn to **131***

368

You keep going farther and farther into the Sandlands until the whole world is nothing but a memory of the ancients. There's nothing out here. Nothing.

You land contemptuously on a large sand dune. A moment later, everything goes black. Giant round maws snap shut around your whole body. Only the very end of your tail remains, twitching on the ground. You've been eaten by something even bigger and hungrier than you.

'Excellent,' the dark-haired Archmage exclaims and claps his hands once. 'Come then. Let me introduce you.'

He proceeds to lead you away from the clear pool by which you landed. Just beyond the next hill, there's a sprawling set of buildings. You can feel a tingle on your scales as you approach it. The place seem to hum with power — that'd explain why your ears are doing just that. There is magic in the air. How could you not have noticed it before?

'Wait here,' Kaheiron tells you and disappears through one of the stout doorways.

You try to stick your snout through the open door, to see what's inside, but the next moment you're almost bowled over by a menagerie of critters of every size and shape imaginable. A small, grey cat uses your snout as a trampoline and bounces over your shoulders, down your tail and up on a nearby wall

'Hey!' you growl at it, but the cat is unperturbed and merely begins washing its face.

Wondering what all these animals are doing here — some, like that armoured, sloth-like creature, don't look like they'd make very good companions for *anyone* — you shoot backwards as a sharp beak clicks shut just inches from your ear.

Returning your attention to the doorway, you realize that you're blocking the exit for a rather regal looking gryphon who clicks their beak at you again. Moving back out onto the grass, you get to watch as several people in robes appear and spend several, rather amusing minutes trying to round them all up and shoo them back in through the door.

How disappointing. There were several interesting looking creatures, including a large, lithe, white fox with blue markings that you wouldn't have minded taking along on your journey.

Eventually, though, you're just left with the gryphon and the cat.

'They're both quite trustworthy familiars,' Kaheiron assures you.

Maybe this wasn't such a good idea after all. You're probably better off alone. You decide the offer. Turn to **174**

*A cat might be handy, you think. It's certainly small enough to carry without noticing. It'll make a good companion. Turn to **195***

*The gryphon holds itself proudly. Watching them, you have no doubt that they'd be able to hold their own in battle. That might come in handy. Turn to **309***

370

Errant blobs of lava fly as the coulee stretches its short neck to the full and bellows like an enraged beast from the netherworld. You waste no time but scrabble as fast as you can back the way you came, tearing at the rock below with your talons.

*It's a close call, but you manage to get away. Looks like the coulee doesn't like leaving its element, for while the volcano rumbles, nothing follows you out. Turn to **225***

*Managing to dodge the rocks and debris falling from the caldera wall as the world rumbles and shifts beneath you is a lot of work, but you jink and weave between the debris like a champion. Turn to **151***

*Unable to get away quickly enough, you narrowly dodge out of the way of the falling rocks, turning to face whatever horror awaits. Turn to **307***

371

It's kind of hard to make out anything: the ocean's constant motions, the way the waves break, the light reflecting off them from the suns. It's all making pinpricks of light dance in front of your eyes.

No, wait — there's something down there after all. You can see it as a bigger light amongst all the others. If anything, it's actually duller than the stars that you're currently seeing.

***Gryphon companion:** Your companion's shrill cries assault your ears as*

*Lightwing tries to get your attention. Turn to **333***

*The light bobs on the water. It's so enticing, you can't take your eyes off it. Turn to **159***

372

You're a dragon. They are insignificant maggots. What are you waiting for? You shake your frills, wondering just that. The last of your human hesitation falls off and you raise your mighty head and roar: defiant, strong and proud.

The battle rages for many days and nights. Then, with a mighty swipe, your talons rake across the battlefield, the warriors and, as it turns out, the dwarf king. It knocks his head clean off, helmet, armour, and all.

But by then both sides are so enraged that you all keep fighting, most of you not even noticing what has happened.

*When things finally settle, it looks like to the victor goes the spoils. Turn to **350***

*Both sides are exhausted. You can keep fighting, but the bigger question is, should you? Turn to **379***

373

'Aaaah!' you shout, then clamp both hands over your mouth. What if someone heard you? Beneath the window, the gryphon shakes their head, fluffing out a few feathers, and keeps watching you with large, soulful eyes.

Oh, no! You never told the Archmage about your world, you realize. You look around your room, wondering how on earth you're supposed to hide a fully grown gryphon on Earth? Lightwing nuzzles you carefully with her beak, burrowing in under your arm and tries to nibble on your ear.

You can't help but laugh, happy to see your companion again, and throw your arms around her neck in a big hug.

374

Adopting a slightly undignified dragonpaddle, as you pass some rocks jutting out of the bottom, something swooshes across your muzzle, slapping you in the face with a tailfin.

Was that a fish?

That *was* a fish. Wait. It couldn't be. It'd be enormous — something that large shouldn't even fit into the lake.

The castle doesn't look like it's getting any closer either. If anything, it now seems further away than ever.

*There's a slight green tint to the water up ahead. It's glowing. It's faint, but it's definitely glowing. Like a tropical beach, turquoise waves mixes with azure. Turn to **315***

*As you contemplate what to do next, a hawk the size of a roc swoops in. You dive deeper, but even from down below you can hear its shrill cries, upset its tasty morsel got away. Turn to **277***

375

Whether or not you return to Kaheiron, you still need to get back to the mainland. The ocean breeze pulls at your sails as you glide effortlessly over the sparkling waters the next morning.

There's plenty of wind to carry you but when you look down, you spot a small fishing vessel that isn't having the same luck. The wind must be moving in layers, for its one square-rigged sail is flapping uselessly.

*You're in a good mood and helping the fishermen won't take much time. Turn to **235***

*Ignore the small vessel and head straight for the Archmage. Turn to **360***

376

As you let out a low roar, something scrambles around, clawing frantically at their surroundings, down there, under the rubble. Shifting some of it, you manage to create an exit space.

*Studying the cat that emerges, the cat looks back at you with solemn green eyes and meows. If you didn't already have a feline companion you do now. Turn to **118***

Cat companion:** Freeing the cat from what remains of the rubble, it shoots off like lightning the moment it's free. Chaos makes a curious noise. You can almost imagine him sticking his tongue out after the departing feline. Turn to **168

*The cat that you find, shakes and shivers the moment you take off. Flying clearly isn't on their top ten list. Might be kindest to find it another home. Turn to **259***

377

Something wells up from deep inside. It flows over you, engulfs you, yet you don't seem to change. At least not on the outside … not yet.

*Gathering yourself together, you turn your eyes to fresh targets. There're cities in this world too, aren't there? They're like concentrated riches — extorted from a people it doesn't belong to. You can think of someone who'd surely be better suited to receive them. Turn to **208***

378

Like a doorway into another world, the hole in the rock feels slightly unreal. It's approaching fast. Too fast. Backwinging furiously, you try to brake in the air. Misjudging the angle, your wings scrape against the rock, tearing against your membranes. You tumble towards the ocean furiously attacking the land beneath. You sink fast, head spinning.

But, against all odds, you manage to pull up at the last minute. Everything stings and, from the ache of it, you've injured at least one wing bone.

*If you expected any sympathy from the gryphons, you're not getting any. Scornful, bird-of-prey eyes flick over you and then you're gone from their thoughts. It's doubtful you'll ever be able to convince them to let you pass the third challenge now. Turn to **172***

379

It proves to be a long and hard battle and by the end of it, neither you nor the dwarves are victorious.

You have slain many of their kind. They have gauged out more than their share of your flesh and scales. The woodlands lie burning beneath you as you heave yourself into the sky with the last of your strength. Below you, the wooden supports in several mines collapse in a cloud of destruction.

*Apparently, the wisdom of dragons comes from long lives of making the wrong choices, you think. It's certainly not in-born. Snorting out some dust, you decide to head for the Sandlands instead. Turn to **332***

*You might not have won today, but you've been growing steadily more worried about what treasures you already own. Best to check in on them first. Turn to **391***

380

Either way. You were there. You figure you bested a whole city. So that counts as a win for you. But where will you go now? You'll have to decide quickly. There's a storm, and it's moving in fast. Faster than you can fly.

*Before the wind catches you, you turn your snout in what you think is the right direction. Turn to **127***

*Before you can make up your mind, the storm is already upon you. Turn to **202***

381

If *you're* strained, its nothing compared to how some of the younger gryphons are feeling by the looks of it. When the leaders eventually level out, you're up so high that you can see not just the island and the sea around it, but several other landmasses as well. But there's no time to admire the view. Everyone is quiet, you realize, because they're all trying to conserve what oxygen they have as long as possible.

Then, the three gryphons that led the climb warble — a sound which sounds very different up here. It must have been a signal!

One by one, the gryphons roll and begin to dive, wings tucked tightly, tightly against their bodies. Faster and faster they go. Turn to **166**

382

The castle is big, but then so are you. It is, however, turning out to be a longer climb than you anticipated. But your effort is rewarded when you spot, still way above you, several windows. These aren't just slits in the stone but supported by proper arches. You attempt to stick your head into the nearest one but your horns keep snagging on the sides.

Pulling back, you peer into the room with one eye closed. It's empty. So are the next two rooms. The third one is filled with some sort of dark, swirling smoke that makes you cough when you breathe it in. The next one again is so bright it almost blinds you.

Once you're finished blinking away the stars dancing before your eyes, it looks like the room is filled with a wide variety of cups and goblets. Gold ones. Silver ones. Crystal ones. Even a couple that look like they were cut from a single ruby almost the size of your paw.

Reaching in with your arm, you can't see which one you want and end up knocking over a whole bunch. Turn to **120**

Cat companion: *Weaving easily between your various spikes and horns, Chaos, who has, up until now, been pretending he wasn't there at all, jumps* *onto your head and meows. Maybe he can retrieve what you came here for? Maybe the cat even knows what you're after in the first place, putting him one step ahead of you. Turn to **165***

*Growling something about never trusting a wizard, you give the castle a mighty smack with your tail. Turn to **111***

383

By the time you return to the challenge, it's already morning. And with daylight's rays, the island at the centre of the lake stands rocky and barren. Of the Castle of Stone, there is no trace. It has returned to whence it came.

*Looks like you didn't succeed. You hope you'll have better luck with the second challenge. Turn to **387***

384

Reluctantly, you leave the pool behind. Glancing over your shoulder one last time, you make your way out of the forest.

*Wondering if those deer-like critters are still out there, maybe you should give them another try? Turn to **107***

*There's nothing for it. You don't feel you can delay any longer. You take a deep breath, steady your nerves and decide to begin your quest for the challenges early. Turn to **200***

385

What looks like a small, brown ball bobs on the surface. The waves wash over it, and, as you keep your distance, not wanting your wings caught in the sea and dragged down, it disappears under the waves. A few heartbeats later and it's back.

From below, you hear a small, weak squeak.

*You hover over the water, uncertain about what to do. Turn to **283***

*It's risky, but you fold your wings and dive towards the ocean with your talons out. Turn to **330***

Gryphon companion:** Before you have a chance to decide what you should do, Lightwing calls out then dives towards the waves. Turn to **248

386

It's nothing less than the strongest of reagents for you. You like a challenge. The more dangerous the better. And it certainly sounds like it'll be dangerous. Dragons are supposed to be impervious to fire, but you're not sure you'd like to test that in a boiling lake of lava.

*Turning your snout into the wind, you take off for the volcano rather curiously named Mt Snag. Turn to **299***

*Maybe opting for the lesser reagent isn't such a bad idea after all, you think. Turn to **222***

387

There's nothing else for it, whatever concoction or contraption the Archmage wanted you to retrieve from the Stone Castle, you'll just have to hope it wasn't an essential ingredient in whatever spell (at least you assume it's a spell, he said he was an Archmage after all) mean to stabilize you.

*Well, that didn't go quite as planned, did it? Maybe you'll have better luck somewhere a little less damp? Turn to **401***

*Now what? Fangs snap shut, scaring the living daylights out of a pigeon that flew too close. You leap into the air to find your bearings. Turn to **340***

388

Before the battle can come to more than cursory blows, you set the forest around you aflame and flee in the midst of the chaos that ensues.

*Besides, you've been growing steadily more worried about what treasures you already own. Best to check in on them first. Turn to **391***

389

It's no effort at all to snatch up the princess. You then dump her unceremoniously back where the unprepared young man is still waiting and go about your way. You've gotten paid already, that's the important part.

*The gold might be impure, but it feels good in your paws. There's not nearly enough of it for your taste. Maybe there's some way of getting more? Turn to **129***

390

There's nothing out here. At least, nothing interesting. You scratch at the ground, fold and unfold wings — enveloping everything in a cloud of fine black particles in the process — and deliver a chagrined roar. While this doesn't deliver a reagent into your waiting paws, it does scare up something small and dusty.

You swing around fast, tail whipping, and down there, something is making a run for it. When you lean down, cutting off its escape route, it falls and tumbles off one of the boulders sticking out of the old lavafield.

Catching an 'Ouch!' from beyond the stones, you peer over the boulder. The traveller jumps in surprise and then, to *your* surprise, swats you on the muzzle with a dusty rag.

*Sitting back on your haunches, you blink uncertainly. What just happened? Turn to **212***

*Dismissing the traveller, maybe you should give the caldera itself more than a cursory look after all? Turn to **204***

This is not *how you should treat a dragon. Turning your muzzle into the air, you stalk off, tail waiving. Turn to **151***

391

As you reach your cave, you sniff the air. You've had visitors while you were out. You carefully search through the entire honeycomb of passages, but find no trace of any intruders. Good.

As time goes on by, you grow increasingly dark in nature and you're soon known as the scourge of the surrounding territory. A plague upon the kingdoms.

Then, the strain of the unharmonized interdimensional quantum hopping takes its toll. Growing ever hotter, day by day, your belly feels as if it's on fire. Soon, you can't even move your frills, not even your talons, without sharp pains causing you to spasm.

You no longer remember much of your old life. If, indeed, you remember it at all, it's just weird dreams to you now. There's no comfort there. No regret. Your final days are agony and you die, alone and soon forgotten. Perhaps the only lasting memory will be your bones, which a merry band of adventurers will, many centuries later, pick up, and which pays them quite a hefty sum of money — dragon bones being a rare find.

392

Still furious, the beat of your wings is hard, powerful, and angry. It carries you far from the place of battle of wills. They can't fly you away from your memories, but that's ok. You don't want them anyway. You shake your head violently, as if trying to dislodge them by force.

*You keep on flying. Turn to **130***

You wonder if there was anything you could have done to have changed *things? The tiniest lingering piece of regret grows stronger the further you fly. Turn to **306***

393

It doesn't look like this path will take you anywhere.

*Kicking up a lot of sand and dust from the bottom of the lake, you growl in annoyance and head back to shore. Turn to **383***

394

You pick one of the tempting, golden fruits and sniff at it. It seems safe enough. Rolling it on your tongue it tastes even better than it smelled. No matter how tempting they are, however, you decide that one is more than enough. These are obviously very special to someone.

*Admitting you shouldn't be here, you decide to return to the dwarves. Turn to **201***

*There's one more place you can try before giving up on the quest. Turn to **299***

395

Few beings have as keen eyesight as a dragon. It's no trouble at all to investigate the dwarven city after dark, you tell yourself. No sense in showing yourself too soon, right?

Curling up in what you deem a secluded spot you fall asleep, dreaming of conquests and challenges vanquished by your might.

*A proper dragon should attack from the sky, but it takes several tries to get back into the air. You're so sleepy. Turn to **400***

When you wake, it takes a while to pull your mind back to the here and now. Best to attack low, you think. They'll never see you coming that way. Turn to **210**

396

The battle is fiercer than you anticipated and you're glad the knight is there — if only to serve as another target. You try to entice the wyrm to abandon its hold on the tree, but though it lunges and spits at you, it never uncurls from the trunk. It's not until both you and the knight join forces that the wyrm finally lies slain at your feet.

Great. Now you just have to figure out how to uproot your *actual* target.

Manoeuvring carefully, it takes all your strength, and some you didn't know you had, before you manage to dislodge the tree from the soil.

Now, though the tree has been felled, the sword is still sticking out of it like a very gleaming, silvery toothpick.

'Pray, beast of the air. Retrieve my sword so that I may continue on my quest!' Sir Chopalot implores you.

This seems a reasonable enough request, you think. Turn to **344**

Grunting something about 'Later!' it comes out as a deep growl. First, you'll need to return to the dwarves, tree, sword and knight, all. Turn to **354**

397

Rolling and twisting in the air, you try to outmanoeuvre the other dragons, but there's nothing you can do. They've flown in these skies for centuries. And while most of them don't seem to possess any magic, those that do, wield it like it's an extension of themselves.

Everywhere you're rocketed by heavy bodies. Slashed by talons. You can't even see anymore, the bursts of flame and fire and ice turning your world into nothing.

One last thought follows you as you fall …

Why?

398

Swooping down, your claws clamour for purchase on part sandstone, part steep roof. Several of the golden tiles fall to the ground. But rather than gold, they're merely gilded copper. How *dare* they trick you like that?

Encircling the tall, round, tower, you roar your defiance. Your tail lashes irritably, knocking the tops off some of the smaller, nearby structures.

You take pleasure in seeing the people below running away.

But that's not the only activity that your presence ignites amongst the elves, humans, beastmen and other puny mortals.

Your sensitive hearing has already picked up the heavy thud of what turns out to be a militia amongst all the shouting and falling debris.

Grinning, you lick your chops in anticipation.

You flare your wings and roar again. Then you leap off the tower, landing with a crashing sound on another building. And another. And another.

Look, the ants can't even keep up with you.

Eventually you grow bored and let them close in. A quick action with your tail sends droves of them crashing into each other, crushed under the weight.

They respond with a hail of arrows which bounce harmlessly against your scales. You'd have thought a place this prosperous should at least have had a decent ballista or two — some sort of large scale defence. This opposition is really beneath your dignity.

They're like pesky flies, really. But they're beginning to annoy you. When you said you wanted tribute, iron and steel weren't what you had in mind. You arch your neck, ready to reduce them to nothing more than ashes. Turn to **218**

Well. This is better. You jump into the fray. Die puny mortals! Turn to ash and crumble before a dragon's might! Turn to **149**

399

Lightwing warbles at you again and you're certain they're grinning. How a gryphon can grin is beyond you, but you'd swear they are. They're also making aerial cartwheels and buzzing you, as if trying to make you go faster.

*Grinning a draconic grin humans would have run a mile to escape, you're just as happy. This is going to be easier than you thought. Turn to **323***

400

The moons are full tonight, so there is plenty of light. You would have preferred total darkness. Dragons see well in the dark. Unfortunately for you, so do dwarves. Looks like you didn't manage to catch them off guard after all.

*Looks like you could do with a bit more time to prepare. Perhaps it's best that you return to your cave and come up with a good plan? Turn to **388***

*Taking one look at the massive surge of bodies coming your way, you pull out all the fierceness you can muster, then turn right around and wing it off into the night. You bet you'll have better luck elsewhere. Turn to **332***

401

You decide to head north, but once in the air, you realize that you don't know which direction is which. You need the map Kaheiron gave you, and to look at that, you first need to land.

Grumbling, you single out a suitable crag rising out of the current forest and land, only to find yourself amongst square stone blocks. Perching on the edge of what must once have been a quarry, you wonder what anyone might have used these for.

*You always imagined these settings, these worlds, to be filled with quaint little villages and rustic towns. Plus a few cities, of course. So far, you've flown over little but tiny hamlets and farmsteads. A disused, overgrown quarry isn't much better. Hardly the stuff excitement is made from. Turn to **146***

402

To your dismay — which result in a large fiery snort from you that sends all the nearest dwarves scuttling out of the way — it turns out that you need to do more than just breathe some flames (not that you actually *breathe* fire, it's more like collecting energy in your maw and it becomes fire as it's expelled).

You'll need to begin with gathering reagents, so that when your flame goes out, the forge remains lit.

It takes quite a while before you get a complete picture of what you're supposed to be looking for, not having any common frame of reference with those doing the explaining. The good thing is it turns out that you have a choice of two.

The lesser reagent proves to be a type of tree. Closely related to the ironwoods you ran into earlier, the dwarves use a special technique to make it burn, but, even with that, it takes a dragon to first set them on fire. All you have to do is find some. Turn to **222**

Not able to tell one tree from another, you opt to go for the stronger reagent; A heart-of-fire. Turn to **386**

403

Your jaws snap shut around nothing. Drats! The bloody wizard — or whatever he called himself — got away. Well, you'll see about that. First, you're going to … but wait. Where are you? You swivel your head, surveying everything around you with lethal eyes.

There isn't any grass or ponds in sight. You're surrounded by steep, barren cliffs. Stretching out your wings knocks them into the stone, scraping the membranes unpleasantly against the craggy rocks.

Your heart seethes as you bend and lick your tongue over what little moisture there is at the bottom of the hole.

For three whole days you claw and scratch at the walls until you finally heave your body out of the trap. Turn to **377**

You curl up at the bottom of the hole, biding your time, and, after two weeks, it dissolves around you. You're free. You run your long tongue over sharp implements of death: Your mind goes through all the ways you're going to make the wizard suffer for making a fool out of you. Turn to **116**

404

Kaheiron raises an eyebrow at the harshness of your voice, but he doesn't say anything. Instead, he merely picks up the chalice, purple crystal, and the bundle of herbs and puts them away.

'Wait!' you protest. 'Aren't you even going to use those?'

Allowing a smile to flitter across his lips, the Archmage can't help but be amused by your reaction.

'I never said you needed to gather the items as if they were cogs in a machine.'

'But …'

'Gathering them did not only give you a purpose while you were here, but they also made you travel to places you would not have visited otherwise and meet people you wouldn't have otherwise met, did they not?'

Grumbling something in reply, for a moment you wonder if you shouldn't have tried to eat the Archmage when you first met him after all.

'Also, they were a kind of test,' Kaheiron admits as, behind him, the cauldron begins pouring its contents into three large steel bowls.

'What? You mean you were watching me this whole time?'

'After a fashion. And before you get all upset over this as I can see you're working your way up to, we had to be certain. You have a good heart and while your human nature causes some confusion for you when in draconic form, you've done well. Well enough that, should you choose to, you're welcome to remain here, in this world. As a dragon *or* as a human, the choice is yours.'

You throw your head up and roar. YES! YES! YES! Turn to **265**

Thinking it over, while being a dragon has advantages you'd actually really like to explore this world in your normal human form. For starters, you'll be able to enter the houses that way. Turn to **192**

'Thanks, but no thanks,' you say. You've had more than your share of adventure for now. Time for something more mundane, like fridges and ice-cubes and something from that hot takeaway that just opened up near the station. Turn to **363**

405

Your gryphon companion squawks and plants herself between you and the first kobold. Wings flared and tail standing on edge, sails spread, they seem to fluff up to twice the size.

You don't think the kobolds would be intimidated, but they do slow down. And after a great deal of whuffing and squawking and high pitched gabbling you don't understand, they retreat, after first collecting their lost comrade.

Hanging your head in shame, you shuffle your feet awkwardly.

Turning around, Lightwing lets you know in no uncertain terms what she thinks of you. Ears burning, as you're trying to work out what to say, you hear the approach of many steel shod feet. Looks like the kobolds weren't the only ones to live in this mountain. Turn to **147**

406

The young man tells you that it's not far, and with your great strides you soon come upon the lair he described.

When he said "lair" you imagined something bleak with a couple of skulls outside and scattered bones having been gnawed on by some great, horrible beast. A mouth into the mountain, dark and forbidding and dripping with stale water and slime.

The mouth of the cave is there, but you wonder if the young man's sense of direction is a little out of date or missing. Where the bleached bones should have been there are a couple of vegetable gardens. Instead of skulls, there are blooming rosebushes and from the cave there wafts the tantalizing aroma of freshly brewed tea.

*But the gardens look like someone has repeatedly trudged through them, and what was once neat flowerbeds have been trampled by heavy boots. Looks like you're in the right place after all. You decide to growl for good measure, drawing out whatever lurks in the cave. Turn to **365***

*Judging by the state of the gardens, you're in the right place. Someone has clearly been here. You'd like a closer look at that cave before deciding what to do next, though. Turn to **224***

407

You snarl and tear after the grey cat at speed. But no matter how you claw the ground or burn the forests, the cat keeps eluding you. Perhaps he was never even there at all.

*After a final fit of rage you take off for more exiting parts, leaving behind you a trail of destruction worthy of a Dark Lord. Turn to **332***

A LEGEND FORGOTTEN, THE DRAGON, HE SLEEPS
BEYOND THESE HILLS, THESE HILLOCKS, THESE KEEPS
SWIFT OF WING AND SHARP OF FANG
THE DRAGON, HE DREAMS OF FIERY DEEDS

Acknowledgements

A great big shout out to all wonderful folks that helped this book into being by believing in it, believing in me or by keeping me sane when the Muse runs off with the cast and throws a party in the mad scientist's lair.

This includes many fellow authors, whether they know it or not lol; my always brilliant editor, Scribecat and some extra brilliant and farsighted backers on Kickstarter, like; Skywings14, Erlinda, Jessie Marston, A. Lachance, Lark Cunningham, Jordan Burattini, Yariloira, Juliane "Nightpark" Völker, Aramanth Dawe, Tysha Dopson, Patrik Andersson, Jeanette Volintine, Tome dragon, Ondrej Zastera, Lisa Spangenberger, Gonçalo Rodrigues, Steven A. Holomshek, Pikey Berbil, Adrianne Compton, Paragrafka, Mark Voss, Danny Tirtosasmito, Laura Norman, Rayen Jonke, Dagmar Baumann, Terramir and Sir Olli.

I had a blast writing this (ok, I also had some moments of thinking my hair would turn grey. If anyone tells you writing a gamebook is easy, don't believe them – all those paths, all those numbers aaaahhh!!) and I hope you will all have even more fun as readers.

I'd also like to thank Steve Jackson and Ian Livingstone for forging ahead back in the day when gamebooks were completely unheard of and giving the rest of us many adventures along the way and as well as a path to follow :)

Chrono-order

Seven of Stars isn't written chronologically, so this is for you if you'd like to read the books in the order they actually take place within their universe.

Remember, you don't *need* to read them in any particular order to enjoy them.

The universe itself is divided into seven different Ages.

1ˢᵗ Age -3ʳᵈ Age

4ᵗʰ Age
"The Damsel and the Dragon"
"Magical Mischief" [**Motionbook]**
"You're a Dragon"

5ᵗʰ Age
"The Dawn of the Winds"
"Wolf's Bane"

6ᵗʰ Age
"The Soul Within" (coming 2019)
"High Fyelds – A New Beginning"
"High Fyelds – The Big Race"

7ᵗʰ Age
"Academia Draconia"

The Damsel and the Dragon

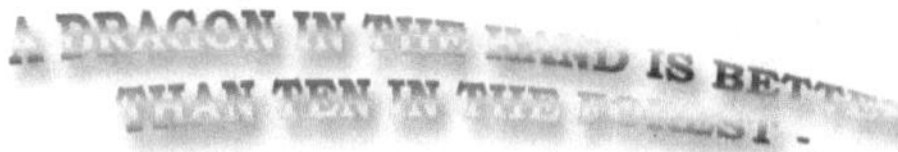

Or so the sages say. Linandra isn't so sure.

Maybe that's because, unlike most sages', Lin's life actually contains dragons. Several of them.

But they don't cause anywhere near as much trouble as the wizards, mages, sorcerers and other arcane users that inhabits her new home.

Welcome to the Twin Towers.

Mae McKinnon

Do YOU have what it takes to face your fears?
THEN JOIN THE DRAGONCORPS
AND PROTECT THE SKIES
OF NEW RETMIA!

Academia Draconia

The school where courage matters!

For Gaile Ashworthey and her fellow students, getting into the Dragon Research Centre had been easy.

. The hard part was staying long enough to graduate.

Trouble is, Gaile has a terrible head for heights. Not to mention, she's not big on teamwork.

But teamwork is what a dragon and rider is all about. If she's going to find a partner, it's going to take a dragon unlike any other.

Mae McKinnon

HIGH FYELDS

A NEW BEGINNING

When Erina has to trade her spaceship for a horse, it opens up a whole new world - literally.

Now she's lost in a place that shouldn't exist. The electronics refuse to work. And there is something lurking in the dark.

It's a good thing the horses seem friendly.

But in Darklight Valley nothing is what it appears to be.

Not the horses.
Not the monsters.
Not even Erina.

Mae McKinnon

DragonQuill Publishing

THE SOUL WITHIN

What they want is a superweapon.
What they need is a miracle.
What they get...

Earth's cities lie abandoned. The people that remain live in vast, subterranean vaults; the last refuges of human kind.

With resources running out, the battle against the alien invaders is periously close to failing.

In this world, a child and a machine dream of soaring through the sky.

Helping writers create clear, concise, and credible work!

This book was made possible with the help of an Editor.

A professional edit is an invaluable resource in preparing a manuscript for print, whether that means sewing up plot holes, tidying up runaway sentences, or catching the last few typos.

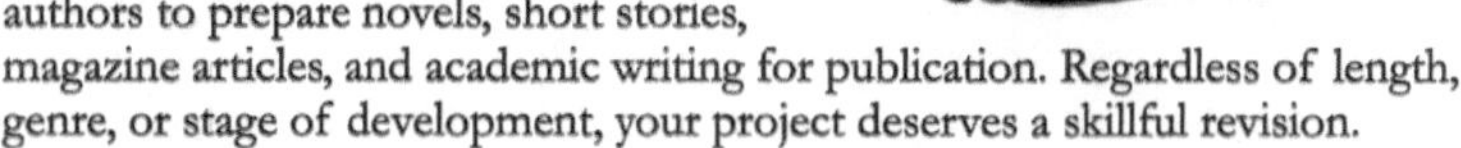

With over 10 years of experience, Ashley Lachance has worked with authors to prepare novels, short stories, magazine articles, and academic writing for publication. Regardless of length, genre, or stage of development, your project deserves a skillful revision.

Have a story or manuscript waiting for a second pair of eyes?

What are you waiting for? Don't pro-cat-stinate!

Check out ScribeCat.ca and get a free quote today!

www.ScribeCat.ca

ashley@ScribeCat.ca

@Scribe_Cat

facebook.com/ScribeCat